MW01600323

To

Love & Hugs
Lyn
2013

Moonbeams

by

Lyn Miller LaCoursiere

Great Books and Novels
Minnesota Authors

Copyright © 2013 by Lyn Miller
LaCoursiere
Printed by Bookmobile
All rights reserved.
No part of this book may be
reproduced without
the written permission of the Publisher.
This is a work of fiction.
Names, characters, places and incidents
are used fictitiously. Any resemblance
to actual persons, events
or locales is entirely coincidental.

Cover photo courtesy of Jack Henneman

Cover design by Genny Kieley
& Lyn LaCoursiere
Format
by Genny Kieley

ISBN # 978-1-938990-99-1

MOONBEAMS

"She was hunted like an animal and now I know I'm next!" Daisy wails to Ed and runs out of the Legion Bar in Birch Lake. He finally catches up with her and takes her to his house, promising she'll be safe. But when the lights suddenly go out in the guest bedroom, she rolls behind the bed clutching her .38 as the stranger treads silently into the room.

"The LINDY LEWIS novels always satisfy my need for good reading and escape from everyday stress. Nightmares and Dreams is storytelling par excellence, creating all the colored threads from which the rest of the novels are woven. I can't wait to read the next book in this new venue."

-Prof. Del Rey Loven

Praises to LYN MILLER LACOURSIERE for putting her flights of fancy to print. We all live vicariously through Lindy and now Daisy, adventurous ladies for sure. We're looking forward to another book by Lyn, but life stops around here when her latest arrives. Then Yogurt and grapes will keep me going until I finish it.

-Judy Anderson

Lyn Milller LaCoursiere's writing just gets better and better in her journalistic ability to entertain. Her Lindy Lewis Adventures stimulates our desire to roam.

-Joe Mostrom, San Jose, Mexico

Books by Lyn Miller LaCoursiere

Nightmares and Dreams

Tomorrow's Rain

Sunsets

Suddenly Summer

The Early Years

Silence

Moonbeams

A note from the Author

I decided to give Lindy Lewis and Reed Conners a little down time, so at this writing we leave them at Reed's home in Birch Lake. However, I may take them out of retirement from time to time, as they often find themselves in situations that do require my attention.

At this time, I'd like you to meet my new character; Daisy O'Dell, who lives in the same town of Birch Lake. Daisy is in her early fifties, single and blonde and financially secure. She left Minneapolis and moved back to her home town several years ago. She is a manicurist with a full house of customers from around the area who love their mani-pedis.

Roma Hurst is her best friend. She is a stoic Norwegian who had moved back to Norway, her homeland, but found she had become too Americanized to stay for long. She has come back to the US to live and to buy a house. Roma is a tall and willowy, boisterous and voluptuous, red head. She's down to earth in her thinking and doesn't hide the fact she loves to cuss.

Daisy and Roma had lived in the same cul-de-sac in Minneapolis years earlier with their young husbands and growing families, and now again, resume their friendship.

I want to thank all of you, my dear friends, for supporting my work. I love writing for your enjoyment and hope you will enjoy this book as these new characters cascade into your living rooms.

You can reach me anytime through my e-mail, or my website. My books are available on line at Amazon.com in paperback and all e-book formats. They also can be found at many book stores in the Minneapolis area and at the Art Center in Maple Grove, MN. Or, you can borrow them from your local library.

Regards always, Lyn

Acknowledgements

I want to thank Judy Ann
and Joyce for their
laborious editing.
Mary M
again for her technical help
and the constant
diligence of my
NIGHTWRITER
friends.

This book is dedicated to
Ella Claire
and
Kaden Christopher,
the new additions to my
lovely family.

-1-

Darkness had come in that far away country, silencing the night creatures in the nearby forest. The moon came out casting a silver sheen on the trees. A mist, soft and white appeared out of nowhere, creeping across the ocean's surface of the now black expanse of water. The gentle swishing of the water muffled the footsteps of a lone stranger walking on the water's edge in the night. Watching and waiting.

***

Daisy O'Dell rushed into her house carrying bags of groceries and plopped them on the cupboard in the kitchen. September was unusually hot and humid this year. She blew her drooping blonde bangs out of her eyes, glanced at the time on the wall clock and saw the plane should be getting close. She kicked off her sandals in the direction of the closet and began to put the groceries away.

After a few minutes she finished in the kitchen, went into the living room and sat down with a sigh. She was tired. The past month had flown by with the excitement of redecorating her house and getting ready. Painters had changed the gray walls to mellow colors of taupe, beige and creams. And new furniture graced the uncluttered living room in light oak wood with soft fabrics and plump pillows. She closed her eyes for a minute and then suddenly fell into an exhausted sleep. She awoke after a few minutes and sat up abruptly. She checked her watch.

Just then the phone rang and she jumped up and exclaimed into the receiver, "Roma, you're here!"

"Mom, it's me!"

"Hi dear," Daisy said to her daughter Val. "I'm waiting for Roma to call from the airport in Minneapolis but she should have been here by now." Daisy's voice faltered.

"Mom, I forgot she's coming in today. Tell her hello and I'll call you later and see when we can all get together."

Daisy put the phone down on the desk and absently straightened the pictures on it. A little stab of anxiety pierced her belly then as she thought of a possible plane crash. But no--, she chased that thought away and looked at her family in various stages of age and dress. We'll have such a good time catching up, she thought happily.

Restless, she went back into the kitchen, and judging the time, the plane should have landed by now. Roma had her cell and they had agreed that she would call just after getting off the plane, before going through customs. Then she would get the rental car and be here in Birch in several hours. And they would celebrate with champagne, steaks and salad.

I can fix the table, Daisy said out loud to ease a bit of her anxiety. Using her good china and candlesticks, she set her table, and then tossed the salad. Now everything was ready and an hour had gone by. Maybe she should change her clothes into something dressier. Roma always traveled looking like an international gypsy, with her high heels and dangling jewelry. Daisy looked at herself in the floor length mirror, at the long skirt with the halter top in gaily colored shades of coral and pink and decided it was good. But she dug out a pair of silver sandals and fluffed her spiky platinum hair, and then clipped on the biggest pair of earrings she could find in her jewelry box.

It's been three years since we've seen each other. Outside of some new wrinkles, I'm sure we don't look too different. Daisy leaned in closer to the mirror over her dresser and checked the lines around her brown eyes, as she rambled on, talking out loud to herself. Another half hour had gone by, making the plane almost two hours late!

She adjusted the pillows again on the couch and closed the blinds against the late afternoon sun. She checked the guestroom, and the new bed-cover and drapes looked inviting. The closet was empty and the dressers were waiting.

Daisy and Roma Hurst had been friends for years. Having met in a neighborhood where they had both been busy with their husbands and raising kids. Now here they were in their fifties, with grown families and single.

Daisy had missed her friend since she had moved back to her homeland of Norway several years ago. Roma had inherited a house from her parents, next to the ocean, and near a forest. The cozy cottage had been painted barn red years ago and now had weathered to a silver gray from the salty breezes. It wasn't big but it was filled with family antiques and the scenery was breathtaking. After a few years of living there Roma found to her chagrin, she had gotten too Americanized to fit in with the old ways of her homeland. That and a tangled love affair had made her decide to come back to America, where she planned to buy a place of her own and settle in.

But where was she now?

Daisy went to the phone and called her cell again which rang and rang. Terribly worried now, she called the airport.

"Flight number 917 came in on time," an agent informed her.

"But my friend was supposed to be on it and she was going to call me when she got in. I haven't heard from her!" Daisy blinked at sudden tears.

"Are you sure you have the right flight?" The agent asked.

"Yes, flight number 917 arriving at five o'clock."

"There is a later flight coming in at nine. Maybe she had a late connection. She could be on that one."

Daisy bit her lip. "Well, I guess all I can do is wait. Thank you for your help." She hung up the phone feeling frustrated. It could happen, she reasoned. And she could just hear Roma cussing about the shortcomings of the travel industry.

She was at loose ends now as dinner was ready and the house in order. She tried to concentrate on television, tried to read and finally at ten she called Roma's cell phone again, then next the airport and was told the nine o'clock flight had come in on time. Now Daisy was really worried.

Maybe there had been a crash somewhere. Or a terrorist attack! Could she have been kidnapped? Daisy sat up with a start as she remembered how Roma always carelessly traveled with thousands of dollars just laying in her purse or tucked in her bra.

Something was wrong. She felt it!

After another call to her cell and still no answer, Daisy called the airport again, intent on finding out something. After long minutes and being transferred to numerous extensions, she finally found someone willing to talk to her.

"There are no more overseas flights coming in tonight," she was told. "But if you will give me the passenger's name," a kindly voiced woman asked after listening patiently to Daisy's worries, "I can do some checking for you if I know where she would have been traveling from. I'll call you back as soon as I know something."

Daisy thanked her and hung up. Twenty minutes later she called back and Daisy held the phone to her ear anxiously.

"The airlines doesn't have a record of a Roma Hurst en route at all on this date."

"But she told me when she was leaving and when she would get here in the US," Daisy protested.

"I'm sorry, but maybe she was delayed and will call you with a later arrival time," the agent replied patiently.

"Maybe, thank you," Daisy murmured and hung up the phone. There had to be an explanation for this, but what? Picking up the phone again she took a chance and dialed Roma's home number in Norway. Hoping to hear her friend's voice and more than likely her cussing a blue streak, that something had definitely gone wrong at the last minute, Daisy waited for the connection. After eight rings, a recorded voice said, "This number is out of service."

Well, that figured. Now what?

She waited well into the night and then finally lay down on the couch and covered up with an afghan. There wasn't anything she could do as she didn't know any of Roma's friends over there.

Should she call the police here in Minneapolis? Should she book a flight to Oslo and report her missing there?

The next day went by and then a week. Daisy was a manicurist and had her own business in the bustling downtown area of Birch Lake. She was hugely successful with her business of faux nails of all descriptions and had the patent of a nail polish she had invented.

Then one day she got a letter. It was addressed to her in Roma's scrawling handwriting. Her hands shook as she tore open the envelope.

"Dear Daisy," it said, "If I don't get to the US, I will probably be dead. I need to tell you about some things, but do not repeat this to a soul. Burn this after you read this."

Daisy read on, holding on to the back of a kitchen chair. Her breath quickened. The afternoon sun had slipped behind a cloud, and tomato bisque simmered on the stove top.

"You see my friend," Roma wrote, "I've gotten myself into some terrible trouble. Just by accident I found out what my old lover does for a living. He's not that affluent business man here with a coin shop as he portrayed himself to me and to the city. He's a hit man known the world over! Daisy, he kills for big money! He's a multimillionaire."

"When I went back to get my things from his house last week, he found me reading a letter that I opened by mistake. When I asked him what it meant, he told me to mind my own business. Well, you know me, I couldn't leave it alone and I found an old acquaintance who is a journalist and she confirmed my thoughts. The man is dangerous and now I know I'm being followed. In our last argument, he yelled 'I'll see you dead before I'll let you leave me!'"

Daisy sat down. It had been a week. Oh Lord, she sat shivering, her heart pounding. Her friend was dead. She knew it!

The days that followed were filled with worry and indecision. She wondered if she should go to Oslo to the police there and tell them her story. But then, it would surely be putting herself in jeopardy. Maybe she'd go anyway!

-2-

Roma heard the footsteps again. Not on the bricked sidewalk that came up to the front of her house from the street, but the soft thudding cadences of sound you make when you walk on the wet packed sand on a beach after the tide has been in. The night was silent and the ocean still as she sat in the dark and listened.

It had been a week since she had gotten out of Gunther Muller's bed. She had confirmed what she had figured out from a letter she found and innocently opened. He had threatened her with death when she had yelled their relationship was definitely over. As he had shouted those hateful things at her, any last feelings she had for him crumbled and died.

She was on her way to the Oslo airport this late night but had to stop at her house to get her passport as she couldn't travel without it. Instead of going back to her house that day he had threatened her, she had driven downtown and circled the blocks in the business district for several hours before she dared stop. She then slipped into an underground parking lot and hid her BMW in a corner, then took the elevator up to the registration desk. She signed RJ Hurst and hurried to the room. This was a discreet B and B located right downtown. Here she stayed for days, using the toiletries supplied. On her way there she had thrown her cell phone in the ocean as she knew he would try to have her traced through it. She had made this reservation to the US months ago and had never told him of it, waiting for the right moment. Now she counted the days until she could get on the flight out of the country and to the US. When she had called a neighbor the woman said strange cars were prowling around the neighborhood.

When Roma had met Gunther Muller a good year ago, he was posing as a coin dealer with his own business in a new and busy mall on the outskirts of Oslo. He was a handsome man somewhere around fifty some years. Those steely blue eyes were what Roma first got hot over as they seemed to see right into her soul, and instantly she knew she was ready for love. And she just let it happen. That first time, she had met him at a party, and when he said "come back to my apartment tonight," and scribbled down an address, she could only follow.

Gunther ushered her into his apartment which was in the elite district of the city. It only allowed the very rich to settle on the hallowed ground, and Roma was impressed, as it usually took a lot to impress her. She had been raised in a house of maids and drivers, and had accumulated quite a portfolio since her marriages had "gone to the dogs" as she said. Now the last years of living alone back in her old country by the sea had cleansed her heart of all the past old hurts. She was lonely and Gunther Muller saw it.

As soon as she stepped over the threshold into his house that first night, he held her in an embrace as he kissed her and began to strip her of all her clothes, and murmured how long he had been waiting for her as he led her to a bedroom. Setting her down on gleaming black sheets, he poured two glasses of wine.

"Roma, I will make you so happy," he said. She had fallen for his smooth talk and his polished moves. This is what she liked in a man. By now she was sitting on his bed, braless, demure in her bikini underwear. Her breasts, "the girls", as she thought of them, proudly stood at attention.

After a few sips of his red wine, he laid her down and gently dripped a few drops over her body. The room was lit by the moon shining brightly through the windows that faced a silent manicured park. Stretched out on his bed, Roma enjoyed every minute of his sensual love-making. From then on a new world opened up for her as he showed her moves she had never known of in her past relationships.

She had been happy and content for months with Gunther. She would stay in his apartment with him, and he would shower her with attention, then he would disappear for weeks at a time. At first, Roma thought he might be seeing another woman and she hired an investigator who reported there was not a woman involved, but that his trips were to countries around the globe like Asia, Paris, Morocco. There the hunt stopped as the investigator couldn't find out anything further. Then she had found that letter and it all led up to now. He was a hired killer and he would kill her too if she left his bed.

He was unaware she had planned to go to the US sometime to visit, but she knew he would have the airport staked out immediately if he found out.

After days hiding in the B and B, she had no choice but to go back to her house as she needed that passport to leave. And on her way to the airport to catch her flight, she stopped and hid her car amongst the alleys and garages and stole silently through her sleeping neighborhood. As she had slipped quietly into her house, that was when she heard the footsteps on the beach just yards away outside. Now she heard them coming closer, swishing through the wild grass on the dunes.

She stood frozen, as she heard keys slipped in and out of the lock on her back door that led up from the beach. Then she heard the door open quietly and felt the air shift in the house. Since she had tossed her cell phone in the ocean, and planned to pick up a new one at the airport, all she could do now to save her life was not move an inch.

She heard him move quietly into the kitchen, and she slipped behind a stuffed chair and crouched down as her heart pounded in her chest. She held her breath as she heard steps leading into the living room. He stood just a few feet from her and now, she could plainly see him in the moonlit shadow. It was not Gunther! But a stocky built man with a hawk like nose and a low forehead. Certainly, she realized then, the svelte gunman wouldn't dirty his hands getting rid of her himself. He would hire it done!

Roma's thoughts ran a mile a minute as she hid behind the chair. Her heart hammered wildly as she could almost feel his gaze fall on the chair, then roam around the room. Finally she heard his footsteps retreat and go toward the stairway. She didn't move an inch until she heard him on the floor above. Then she slipped silently to the desk across the room, grabbed her passport, and tiptoed out the back door.

It was still dark and she ran, ducking behind trees and shrubs and got back to her BMW. She had purposely left it unlocked and now climbed in and was out of there in minutes.

She caught her breath. She could have used a phone and called in and changed her reservation to the US, but waiting the week out hopefully was a good idea.

At the airport she parked the car in long term parking as she had arranged earlier with the rental agency and took a bus to the terminal. Standing in line waiting to board, with her dark glasses on and a scarf covering her flame colored hair, she suddenly felt something jab her in her back and a voice whisper, "Don't breathe a word. Turn around and walk away with me. I've got a bomb on me and if you try anything, my boss, your lover, will push a button and blow us all up in this place!"

Roma's stomach lurched. Not now, when she was almost on the plane. She tried to make eye-contact with the attendant checking boarding passes a few people ahead, but she was busy with the passenger's right in front of her. She felt another sharp jab in her back. This time it felt like a knife cut through her clothes.

"You got one second to start moving." She could smell the man's musky sweat and now she could see him out of the corner of her eyes.

"Screw you, you asshole," she whispered. "I'm not going anywhere but on this plane."

"Believe me woman, your old lover has got me wired and if I don't bring you out in another five minutes, he will push a button and we along with all these lovely travelers will be toast!"

Roma felt her heart rate thunder in her chest, and her stomach plummet.

What the hell, her thoughts racing, she still had minutes! Maybe he was bluffing and she was a gambler! And standing there with her back to him, she rammed her elbow back into his solar plexus, swung around on her right and jammed two fingers straight into his eyes and then kneed him in his crotch. All fluid moves she had learned years ago in a defense class.

"Ahh--," he groaned out loud for a long moment and then sagged to the floor clutching himself. Roma yelled, "He's got a bomb!" In the instant confusion as people fought their way out of the crowd, she darted behind the ticket taker who had stepped away from her stand, and slipped her pass through the machine and ran into the plane just before the doors slammed close. She had slid off her dark glasses and the scarf covering her red hair as she ran. Inside the plane she found her seat and forced her breath to slow, and this all took place in scant minutes.

The plane had sat revving its engines and then apparently the pilots got the message to "get the hell away from the building," just as she was banking on. She knew from experience what would happen as she had been a flight attendant in the US for a few years.

She quickly darted in the restroom and slid a white tam like cap over her red hair and added her granny glasses to her new look, and then slipped on two outfits she had in her carry-on bag. Her seat was amongst a family traveling with kids and relatives and soon the plane soared out of Oslo, Norway.

It was a nine hour trip with a stop-over in Iceland. Not wanting to call attention to herself, she moved with the families as they shopped for souvenirs. Hours flew by then and soon they landed in the US at the Minneapolis/Saint Paul terminal. Roma hurried through the busy concourse in her granny look, and outside to hire a car. By now it was late afternoon in the city and shoppers were clamoring for the fastest routes to get away from downtown. Roma joined the mad rush, but not without a constant eye on the road behind her. It was another two hour trip to Birch Lake and now the further she got on her journey, the safer she felt.

Soon the little town where her dearest friend Daisy O'Dell lived came into view and she blew out her breath and relaxed.

-3-

Daisy O'Dell was tired and cross this afternoon. It was a Saturday in the small town of Birch Lake and the Labor Day holiday week-end. She hated long weekends. If she could, she would just keep her shop open and stay busy. But of course her customers all had families and plans. She had a family too, but her kids all lived in the big cities and had their own thing going. If only Arch, this new interest she'd found on the web-site would call her. But he had stated on his ad he was looking for someone not older than forty. She had lied and said coincidently, "that's my age!" on their last e-mail. But could he tell from her pictures that she had subtracted a few years? Alright, admit it was ten! On the photo's that he'd sent to the "lonely hearts club" web-site, the old dude looked to be in his late sixties or even early seventies.

Daisy had been adding the finishing coat of polish to a customer's acrylic nails who had been talking about her troubles finding that special one to take her away. A few minutes later as Daisy came out into the small waiting area to collect her next appointment; she saw this stranger wedged in amongst her regular ladies. She said "I'm sorry, you must be new? Would you like an appointment?"

"Hello Daisy," the lady said.

"What can I do for you?" Daisy asked and then looked at her. The woman looked to be from another part of the world in her odd clothes as it looked like she had several layers on.

Then whipping off the white knit cap and granny glasses and fluffing her wild red hair, Roma held out her arms. "Daisy, it's me!"

'For God's sake," Daisy managed to say after she was smothered in the embrace. "I thought you might be dead," she whispered. Her face was pale.

"Daisy, I thought I would be too." Roma exclaimed.

Daisy stepped back, "I got your letter and tore it up as you said, but I didn't know what to do." She whispered, "I even thought I should fly to Oslo and report you missing."

"I've been hiding out, Daisy, as I told you when I sent that letter, he threatened to kill me!" Roma put a hand over her lips to stifle her outburst.

"I'll just be a minute," Daisy told her waiting customers and took Roma's arm and led her out of the waiting room and into the back area. Here the room had a colorful burst of coral on the walls and pink and cream on the furniture. The fumes still lingered in the room from the acrylic nails Daisy had just finished, and Lady Gaga was still telling her man to "hit the boards".

"Oh my God Roma, I've been so worried." Daisy said tearfully and her voice shook as she went on, "It's hard to believe Gunther is a hit man. He seemed so normal when I met him that time!" She wiped tears from her eyes now as they stood.

"I know and I thought he was such a good catch." Roma pulled Daisy close again and they hugged. "And what a devious fool he is and stupid me, for not seeing through his web of lies." Roma stepped back and began unzipping her shirt.

"Cripes, I look awful. I've got all these clothes on.

Daisy put a hand over her lips and almost giggled and said, "I wondered."

"Let me tell you, I traveled in disguise. I slipped these outfits on when I got on the plane. I had taken these in my carry-on and see, I added another hundred pounds!"

Daisy watched in disbelief then as she stepped out of a fleece lined sweat suit, a bulky sweater and knit pants and then stood in tight legged jeans and a long shirt.

"You see," Roma went on, "his men would have been looking for a slim red head to deplane in Minneapolis, not a two hundred pound old lady wearing a granny cap and glasses." Roma opened her purse then and took out a bag and large mirror and began putting on her make-up.

Daisy just stood speechless and watched her friend.

"Cripes, girlfriend, say something!"Roma laughed and looked around for a seat.

Daisy managed to finally get herself under control but still felt shaky from the excitement. "Here sit." She pointed to her small desk in the corner of the room.

"I was watching behind me on the road coming here too just in case I was being followed!" Roma went on and expertly creamed her face and spread foundation. Then in short minutes she had applied lipstick, blush and mascara as she brought Daisy up to date on her journey.

"Do you think you really got away from him?" Daisy asked.

"I do. In that scuffle I brought about when I was getting on the plane in the Oslo airport, I'm sure whoever that was threatening me with a bomb, thought that I had escaped in the crowd!"

"A bomb? My God, Roma," Daisy swallowed hard over her nerves. Since leaving Minneapolis years ago and moving back to her small town where she had grown up, her life had become pretty low-key. She felt safe back among her many relatives and friends and was even bored at times. But now having her best friend here sent rivets of excitement through her. And a little fear! It wouldn't be long though, before news of this mysterious frumpy woman who had come into Daisy's shop would spread throughout the community and set tongues wagging.

"Roma," she said now, "go to my house while I finish up here with my ladies. The key is under the red pot of geraniums standing next to the back door." She ran a hand through her spiky blond hair and smoothed her pink nylon uniform. Her backless high heeled wedgies whispered on the tiles as she helped Roma gather and fold up all the clothes she had tossed on the floor in the excitement.

"Okay. Thanks girlfriend." Roma yawned, "If you don't mind, I'll take a nap in that new guest room!"

"Make yourself at home and help yourself to whatever looks good in the fridge. I'll be home in a few hours." Daisy walked with her back through the front of her shop and waved as she left.

Almost a decade had gone by since Daisy and Roma had left their respective neighborhoods in Minneapolis. Daisy's five kids had left home and gone to colleges and then struck out on their own. When the chaos in her house had settled finally, her husband and she had realized they didn't have anything left together and split. They had sold the family home and divided their finances and Daisy had given Minneapolis the finger and moved back to her old hometown. Here her money went far as she bought a house and a shop and opened her business. Now she was well known about town and respected. Although Birch Lake was only three hours away from Minneapolis, she didn't go back often. But now and then she would go and visit friends and catch up with some of her kids. She always breathed a sigh of relief though as she left the teeming metropolis of the city for the picturesque peaceful life at the lake.

Now she sped through Main Street in Birch Lake in her silver Porsche to the edge of town and over several blocks to her house.

Daisy loved her home. It was a three bedroom ranch built with tan bricks. It was several decades old when she bought it and she had totally renovated the inside. Now it had gleaming cherry wood cupboards and woodwork, marbled white granite counter tops and wood floors. Glass doors opened to a bricked patio and a swimming pool. Her landscaping had been professionally done.

Actually, when Daisy O'Dell had come back home, she was almost considered a celebrity by some of her town folk. Honestly, some of the stories that had filtered back had made her out to be an actress, and some had even heard she had spent time in Hollywood. Also, they heard she was a model for this famous outfit down there.

The talk kept the town busy for years as her legendary life was discussed and embellished, and some of it was true. Senior citizen Otto would sit at the counter in the Woodsmen Café in Birch Lake, in his bib-overalls with his favorite Old Spice after shave fragrance permeating the air and chat with Flo, the waitress and the other senior citizen. And when Daisy came back to live amongst them they were almost giddy with excitement as she made over the old McNelly house on the corner and made it into a show-place. Then, adding a swimming pool, no less, and one of those lanais that they all wondered about. When she opened her business, the town ladies clambered to get their fingers and toes done and thank goodness, they kept coming back.

Daisy parked the silver Porsche in the garage and went into her house. She stopped dead in her tracks when she came into the kitchen and saw Roma on the floor. Still as death!

-4-

Daisy dropped her purse and knelt on the floor at Roma's side. Her red hair fanned out around her face.

"Roma, what happened?" Daisy shook her. "Open your eyes," But Roma just lay there pale and unmoving as Daisy franticly searched around the room for some clue as to why her friend had collapsed. Then remembering she had some smelling salts in the first-aid box, she hurried to her closet and grabbed the vial. It took just a minute as she waved it under Roma's nose for her to come to and sit up. Roma scrambled to get up from the wood floor in her friend's kitchen.

"Daisy," she yelled, "we've got to get out of here!" The black sweater and pants outfit was twisted on her, and the long gold and silver scarf lay in a pile on the floor.

Daisy could only gawk at her friend.

"Come on Daisy," Roma whispered, taking her arm and pulling her along to the door.

"Wait a minute," Daisy protested.

"Daisy, listen. I found a snake in my suitcase. And this isn't the average garden snake that I'd find around my grounds at home." Roma looked around the kitchen frantically.

"Well for God's sake, a snake is a snake." Daisy said and jumped up on a chair, and Roma followed. "No, that's not so, listen to me Daisy. This was one of those red and white striped poisonous ones you only see in a zoo!"

"You had that in your suitcase?" Daisy asked and her face paled.

"I opened it to hang up my clothes," Roma said as she balanced on top of another chair. "What do we do now?"

"I don't know, but we have to find it!" Daisy had carried in Chinese dinners for them and had sense enough to put them on the cupboard when she first came home from work and not dropped them when she saw Roma on the floor. She had planned on opening a nice bottle of wine to go with their meal. She tucked her pink nylon uniform around her knees now as if that would keep the reptile away, then stepped down and slid into her wedgies which lay on the floor.

"Roma, come on. We have to get out of here! How the hell could you have a venomous reptile in your suitcase?" She yelled as they ran out the front door.

Roma tossed her long red hair. "I know he hired someone, the bastard!"

"Who," Daisy asked, "You mean Muller?"

"Yes, who else. Oh God, I wonder when he got in my house at home?" She shivered. "Daisy, I can't remember if I left the top of my suitcase open. It's out and loose by now. Oh God," she whispered, "What will we do?"

By now Daisy had her wits about her. "I'll call the police and they'll come over and find it." While she talked, she looked around nervously on the porch and lawn for this red and white striped snake and then opened her cell phone.

"Erma, this is Daisy O'Dell. I need some help here!" Erma had been the dispatch operator for the Birch Lake Sheriff Department for years and between her and Sheriff Monte they seemed to keep the crime rate low. There hadn't been much going on until the drowning of those two boys from across the Mexican border last year. And that had made the national headlines and rocked the community to its roots.

"Daisy, what on earth is the matter?" Erma asked.

"A friend of mine has come from Oslo to visit, and she found a dangerous snake in her suitcase!" Daisy's nerves now were making her voice crack under all the nerve-racking confusion.

"Did you say a snake, Daisy?" Erma questioned.

"Yes, it's one that has red and white stripes."

"Okay, stay put and I'll send the Sheriff over." Erma immediately found him at his house, ready to sit down to a nice supper with his family.

Five minutes later, in the small town of Birch Lake, the sirens blared and lights flashed on the brown LTD. Sheriff Monte hadn't had a chance to use all that flash and dance for a long time and now he smiled to himself as he sped through town.

But how in the world would he catch a snake? He took out his cell and called his deputy. "Gordie," he said, "turn on that computer of yours. I got a snake that has red and white striped skin. Find out how to kill the bastard, and then come over to Daisy O'Dell's house!"

Pulling up to Daisy's driveway, he checked his defensive tools.

He had his gun and his aim was known the county over. Whatever else he needed he didn't have a clue. A club and a rope?

Daisy ran over to his car as soon as he stopped.

"Sheriff," she said breathing hard, "I hope you can catch this thing my friend found in her suitcase."

"What the hell. Where did she get this snake, you said?" Sheriff Monte was breathing hard.

"She doesn't know. She just got here from Oslo."

"Did you say Oslo, Norway?" Sheriff Monte asked.

"It was in her suitcase." Daisy clasped her arms around herself to ward of the shivers as they walked to her house. "We don't know if it's still inside it or if it's loose around in the house."

"God almighty," was all he could say.

Daisy led him up to join Roma on the porch of her house. "This is Roma, my friend from Norway."

After a quick exchange of greetings Sheriff Monte asked. "How and where did you pick up this snake?"

Shaking her head, Roma said, "It was put in there to send a message."

"A message, from whom?" The sheriff asked dumbfounded.

Daisy could see it was time she stepped in. She smiled and took Roma's arm. "My friend sees ghosts at times. We just need to find it and get rid of it!"

Just then Deputy Gordy came flying down the street with lights and sirens blasting through the whole neighborhood. Cars filled with curious residents followed close behind him.

"Boss, boss," we have to quarantine the area," he yelled as he got out of the LTD, his beige uniform sagging on his lanky frame.

"God almighty Gordy, what the hell are you talking about?"

Deputy Gordon hurried up to the porch and handed Sheriff Monte a bat. "I figure we'll corner it and I'll throw this sack over it and nab it." He demonstrated this action to the sheriff.

Daisy and Roma stood off to the side of the porch while this was going on.

"I can't believe all this Roma," Daisy said. "For God's sake, at least you closed the door and got out of the bedroom before you fainted."

Roma had gathered her flaming red hair and knotted it on top of her head. "My only thought was to get the hell outside fast, but I guess I lost it before I got very far."

"Come on, let's go and sit in my car. It's getting too chilly to stand here any longer."

"We'll be in my car," Daisy said to the sheriff, and she grabbed Roma's arm and they hurried over to her Porsche and slammed the door.

"Daisy, I'm so sorry, but I can't set foot in your house until that monster is gone," Roma whispered, then went on, "Cripes, I knew something gross would happen sooner or later!"

-5-

The quiet neighborhood at Daisy O'Dell's house had suddenly erupted in commotion as Sheriff Monte waited for Deputy Gordy.

"Did you find out what to do? What the hell kind of snake is red and white?" The sheriff shouted. He was still breathing hard.

"Here's what I found, boss," the young deputy said. "It's called a red racer and it's found in the warmer countries."

"Well hell, I gathered it's new to this part of the country. Did you find out how we get it?" Sheriff Monte's voice echoed over the front yard.

"We have to catch it and put it in a sack." Deputy Gordon said as he carried a baseball bat, a tennis racket and gunnysack. "I got these out of the garage, but this is all I could think of to bring. We don't ever have anything like this, boss."

"God almighty," Sheriff Monte mumbled under his breath as he looked around at all the hubbub. The street was lined with cars now and the residents were edging closer. Stan from the Woodsmen café was there, still wearing his white apron. Even Otto, the town senior, was there and leaning on the arm of the bartender from the Legion Club. Folks didn't worry about leaving their businesses open, as there was always trusting customers willing to take over if necessary.

Deputy Gordon hurried up to the porch and handed Sheriff Monte the bat.

"I figure we'll corner it and I'll throw this sack over it and nab it."   He demonstrated this action to the sheriff.

As Daisy and Roma sat in Daisy's car and waited, occasional whoops and hollers erupted from inside the house. The women looked worriedly at each other. Daisy shook her head and worried that in their exuberance, if they were wrecking her house. And if Roma, would have to thrown away all her belongings.

Soon all the commotion stopped as Deputy Gordon stepped out on the porch holding the squirming gunny sack away from his body.

"We got him," he yelled. "It's a mean one and probably a foot long." He went to his Ford and put it in the trunk.

Sheriff Monte came out of the house then and Daisy got out of the car and ran to him. "We had to move some furniture, but nothing's ruined, Daisy," he said wiping his brow.

"What will you do with it?" She asked, as Roma joined them.

"I'll give that place in Minneapolis a call. It's a zoo, I think." He was still breathing hard and the back of his shirt was wet with sweat. "I'll need you to come down to the station and make a statement, for the record of course."

"Can that wait until tomorrow? I've haven't had a chance to settle my company in yet." Daisy smiled at Roma.

"Sure, no hurry." On the way to his vehicle, Sheriff Monte said to the nearest residents, "We got it so you can all go home now." But the people stood for minutes longer and discussed the event to the fullest.

Daisy and Roma went in her house and closed the door.

"Now I think the first thing we have to do is drink this bottle of wine I've been cooling." Daisy proclaimed and busied herself gathering glasses and an opener. "Come on, girlfriend, let's go out to the lanai and put our feet up. If we're not at a pleasant place after we finish this bottle, I've got more." And they both walked through the house out to the lanai. Not too much damage had been done except some rugs were tossed around and the chairs around the dining room were standing askew.

Roma had draped her gold and silver scarf around her neck and as they walked, she tucked her shirt in. She had grabbed up her purse from the cupboard where she had put it earlier and hung it over a shoulder. "Thank God, I've got most of my make-up in here." She took out a compact when they got to the lanai and scrutinized her face for damages.

"You look just fine now Roma, but good Lord, you were pale as a ghost when I found you on the kitchen floor."

Roma busily puffed blush on her cheeks, then more color on her plump lips.

After giving herself a practiced once over in her mirror, she sat back.

"That monster tried to kill me, Daisy," Roma exclaimed. "And I'm sorry for disturbing your whole town."

Daisy poured two glasses of the wine and handed one to Roma. "Don't worry about it," she laughed, "we needed something to liven up the place."

"Isn't it a holiday here in the US?" Roma sipped her wine.

"It's Labor Day weekend." Daisy kicked off her wedgies and put her feet up on an ottoman. Her tanned legs were trim and muscled from her dedicated exercising. She checked her pedicure and saw her part-time manicurist had done a good job on her toes the other day.

"How do you celebrate this holiday?" Roma asked as she pulled off her high heeled sandals.

"It's strictly small town stuff here. There will be a lot of boats out on the lake and campers in the park."

Roma put her bare feet up on the ottoman and she noticed Daisy looking at them.

"Well, I didn't have time," she remarked defensively, "I figured I could get a mani-pedi here in your shop." They laughed.

The two friends sat together out on the lanai enjoying their wine and each other's company. They didn't see the red racer's mate as it circled curiously through the house and out to the lanai in its search for a new home amongst the cool lake weeds and towering oats that bordered the beaches of Birch Lake.

-6-

When Daisy and Roma had finished that first bottle of wine, Daisy walked barefoot into the kitchen and to the wine cooler that was built into her cupboard and picked up another of the fine wines. She expertly uncorked the bottle and hurried back to her guest. Roma had opened the waistband on her slacks and sat back comfortably on the pillow covered rattan couch.

The sun had gone down sending a rainbow of colors over the lake and soon a full moon descended over the placid mirrored surface. A slight breeze moved through the screened lanai taking the smoke from their cigarettes away from the house. Actually, both women only smoked on special occasions and of course this was one. Daisy had found a long silver holder in a drawer and even had an extra one for Roma who blew plumes of smoke out that disintegrated out in the evening breezes off the lake.

Roma asked curiously after a minute. "Daisy, I have to ask you, whatever made you give up you life in Minneapolis?   Don't get me wrong, your home is beautiful, but I've always wondered what made you make such a drastic change?"

A frown spread over Daisy's face and she nodded her head. "It was a sudden decision. And I've never told anyone this, and I don't know if I can talk about it now." She ran a hand through her blonde hair with one hand. Her lips tightened.

"Was it a man?" Roma asked, not able to keep the curiosity out of her voice.

Daisy took up her glass of wine and sipped thoughtfully. She looked at her friend, her best friend. But she wasn't sure she was ready to share this with even her.

"Oh shoot, I'm sorry," Roma went on, "Me and my big mouth!" And she leaned over and clutched Daisy's hand with hers.

Daisy had a minute to gather her feelings and now with the added wine for courage she took a drag of the Marlboro.

"Years ago, is it almost ten?" The two women looked at each other and nodded in agreement at the number of years that had gone by already. "Roma, you had moved back to Norway. I was alone, totally alone. My kids had grown and moved on, my marriage was over and my home was gone. One day I woke up and when I realized that everything was gone, I panicked. Although, I was financially well off after the sale of the house and splitting up our portfolio. And it was a man, Roma!"

"Oh cripes Daisy, what happened?"

"I did such a stupid thing! I'm embarrassed to even talk about it now."

"Well, for God's sake, what the hell did you do?"

"I bought a man!" Daisy said.

Roma looked at Daisy. "You bought a man? How did you do that?"

Roma's face was flushed.

Daisy instinctively put her arms around her chest in a protective manner and wondered if she could admit to the whole story. Then thought, why not, Roma is my best friend.

"Yup, I bought a man," Daisy said. "I put an ad on one of those web-sites on the internet and I got one!"

"A man?" Roma was almost ready to laugh again but saw that Daisy had a sad look on her face, and then blew another plume of smoke from her cigarette toward the screened roof in the lanai.

"You know I was so vulnerable. I fell head over heels in love with this guy and soon I was giving him money!"

"Oh, Daisy!"

"I did. It started with me paying for an evening out now and then. Then I bought him a car. I woke up when he wanted me to loan him money to buy a bar."

"A bar?"

Daisy lit another Marlboro and her hand shook as she stuffed it into the holder. "Listen to this," she went on, "he claimed he could work without pay and in no time reimburse me. I was doubtful but almost ready to do it. Roma, I'm talking about two hundred grand. Then just by accident, I ran into an acquaintance who knew him. I found out then he was a well known womanizer, and, he had a history of using other women before me."

"Did you lose a lot of money?"

Daisy grimaced. "About five thousand. Then I stole the car back, the jewelry and the clothes. You know, Roma, I taught that asshole how to dress and how to act in public. All he had going for himself when I first met him was a big cock!"

Both women howled with laughter at that and then sobered after a minute and Roma shook her head. "Fucking men! I swear I'll never fall for another." She bit down on her lips as Daisy went on.

"That's one reason I moved. I needed a whole different look on life." Daisy ran a hand over the flowered cushion on the couch. "You know when I left Minneapolis I got rid of everything I owned, even my furniture. I only took some of my clothes."

"Daisy, you're lucky he's not stalking you!" Roma had opened the top of her slacks that had been binding her waist and now she untucked her shirt.

"I haven't heard anything about him for a few years now, but he's probably in jail or has been run out of town by now." Daisy laughed then, feeling relief she had shared this embarrassing epic of her life.

"I wish I could say that about my latest fling," Roma said shaking her head. "To think Muller wanted me dead! A man I loved. A man I had sex with every which way. Fuck, we women are so stupid at times. Damn it, I have such a headache!" She took the clip out of her hair and shook out her red tresses. "And putting that snake in my suitcase I could have been dead by now!"

Both women were quiet for a minute as they thought about the horror of this reptile clamping its jaws on their person and spitting its deadly venom into their bloodstream.

Daisy sat up abruptly and shivered, "Damn, girlfriend," she whispered, "let's go into the living room. It's getting spooky out here now that the sky has clouded over." And they picked up their glasses and smokes and Daisy slammed the door to the lanai shut. But the abrupt noise awakened the red and white racer that had circled around the house and settled in the corner of the lanai in the basket of colorful yarns where Daisy kept the afghan she was knitting for the church bazaar. It lifted its arrow shaped head over the edge and searched its surroundings for danger with its darting poison laced tongue.

The next day of the Labor Day week-end was a Saturday and Daisy and Roma sat in the sunny kitchen. This morning the house smelled delicious from the aroma of fresh coffee and the apple cinnamon toast they were buttering. Daisy had a short red terry cloth robe tied around her waist and Roma had borrowed a zebra striped lounge coat from her.

Daisy's blond hair was straight and still wet from her shower. She didn't weigh more than a hundred and fifteen pounds and today, with her face devoid of any make-up, from a distance she looked like a skinny boy.

"Did you sleep well?" She asked Roma. "I bought a new mattress set for that room."

"Hmm-, after I took my pills, I slept like a rock." A tremor shook through her shoulders then as Roma clutched her coffee cup, "But until then I had the hibbe jibbes."

-7-

"Let me take you out and introduce you to my friends and folks around town," Daisy said to Roma as they drank their coffee the next day while sitting in the sunny kitchen. After the two bottles of wine they had consumed the night before, they both were moving pretty slow.

"Okay," Roma agreed. "But where should we go?"

"There're only two meeting places in town where you can meet most all the residents." Daisy laughed.

"Where?" Roma asked.

"The Legion club and the Woodsmen Café," Daisy said as she poured more coffee. She took a bottle of orange juice, a jar of jam and a plate of butter from the refrigerator, then placemats and napkins from a drawer in the cupboard and set them all on the table.

"We've got quite a few colorful people here and you've got to meet Otto and Flo. They're somewhere in their nineties and you'd think they were thirty years younger. I guess I've never heard their last names. Otto never misses a day uptown. He'll start out at the Café for breakfast and then go to the Legion to be the first customer when they open."

Daisy checked the toast and saw it needed more time and went on, "He has his own bar-stools in the places and he'll stay at the Legion all day, eat a burger for dinner and greet the evening crowd, then leave about 8 o'clock. He knows everyone and everything. This old guy always wears a striped bib overall, a plaid flannel shirt and a necktie. He must have hundreds of feed caps that he wears over his bald head, has a walrus mustache and always leaves a trail of Old Spice fragrance.

Roma spread butter on the toast and brought it to the table and sat down.

"They sound a lot like some of my relatives back home. In my country longevity is the norm. It's all the fish we eat, they say."

"Hmm-I've heard that too." Daisy remarked and took a drink of her coffee and went on, "Then you've got to meet Flo who is around the same age. She's a waitress at the Woodsmen Café and has been there for decades. She never misses a day. And you'll never find a gray hair in her red French twist and her white uniform and crepe soled shoes are spotless."

"Do these lovely people have family close by?" Roma asked curiously.

Daisy stood still for a minute as she bustled around in the kitchen. "I guess I don't know," she said. "When I think about it I've never heard anything mentioned about families."

"Sounds like you have some interesting people here." Roma said and attacked her toast after slathering on loads of strawberry jam.

Daisy had turned on the radio that stood on the cupboard for a Saturday morning show and now a melodious accordion started the program with a toe tapping waltz.

"This is my two brother's show," she said. "Listen, this is our families tune. Our grandfather wrote this when he was alive. He played the violin." Daisy waltzed a few steps around the kitchen as she came to the table carrying more toast.

Roma watched her and laughed.

"My brothers Richard and Eddie are well known around the country, and I go to some of the places they entertain at," Daisy said and put her feet up on the next chair, sipped her coffee and laughed. "And Roma, I can dance all night with my relatives. That's another reason I moved back, I feel safe living here!"

"You're so lucky, Daisy, after my sister died, I didn't have anyone except my sons, of course. And they didn't want me around."

Daisy looked at her friend curiously. "I've never understood that. Why ever not?" She asked.

Roma shook her head. "It's a long story and I'll tell you about it sometime. But it started when my youngest married that awful woman!"

"I thought you liked her? Ivory, isn't it?" Daisy asked.

"That's the witch's name. I never even told them I was moving back here again." Roma looked around. "Damn, I could go for a smoke."

"Well, we're not having any; it's too early. Here, have more toast!" Daisy advised and Roma took another slice and the moment passed.

"Roma, I emptied the chest of drawers and the closet for you in your room. Do you want me to help you unpack this morning?" Daisy asked.

Roma put the toast down and wiped a crumb off her lips. "Cripes, I didn't even open it. That's why I had to borrow this robe of yours!"

Daisy looked at her and then did a double take. "You didn't?"

"I couldn't, I've got to get rid of it. Everything! Have you got a big garbage bag?" Roma asked, "I'll just slide it in there and put it in your garbage can! Daisy, that snake lived amongst my clothes and things for several days." Roma whispered and shivered. "I can't wear anything, or use anything in there."

"Oh for God's sake Roma, you can dry clean all your clothes."

"No, no," Roma exclaimed. 'I can't wear those things again. It's good I was wearing all my good jewelry, and then, if you remember I was wearing a couple outfits when I got here!"

"But Roma, you can't do that, throw all your things?" Daisy said shaking her head. "That's unheard off."

"Well now you've heard it!" Roma said getting up from the table and looking around the kitchen. "Where do you keep your garbage bags? I'm going to do it right now."

Daisy went to a drawer and pulled out a black garbage bag and handed it to her.

The two women went down the hall and into the guest bedroom. It was a lovely room painted a soft sage, with cream colored drapes and carpet and furniture. The bed was a double size and was perfectly made up with the toss pillows in exactly the same place as before, Daisy noticed. Roma's suitcase sat on the same stool untouched.

Roma marched over and slipped the bag around it and held the ends together. "Now show me the way to the garbage," she exclaimed, "the sooner we get this out of the house, the sooner we can relax."

Daisy was at her wits end, after the commotion last night when the cops came, plus the whole town. She could only shake her head in dismay over it all now and lead the way to the garage.

"Roma, where did you sleep last night? I could see you didn't spend any time in that bed?" She asked now after coming back into the kitchen.

Roma laughed. "Cripes, I didn't want you to know, but I took a blanket from the linen closet and went back out to the lanai. I just got the hibbie jibbies being so close to where that killer snake was." Not knowing she had spent the night just a few feet away from that killers mate who had made its home in Daisy's basket of yarn and the unfinished afghan.

"I don't know how you're going to manage not having your things, Roma. But you can use anything of mine you need."

"I'm thinking I'll drive to Minneapolis one day soon and go shopping. I need new clothes anyway." They were standing in the kitchen talking now.

"Let's get ready and go uptown," Daisy said.

Several hours later, Daisy and Roma entered the crowded Legion bar. Conversation halted for minutes as the locals looked Roma over good seeing she was an outsider, but as she was with Daisy, one of their own, they accepted her into their inner circle.

Two men sitting at the bar gave up their seats for the women. By now there was a line-up of two to three customers deep around the bar, even though it was early afternoon, and the beginning of the Labor Day holiday.

The juke-box had been filled with quarters earlier and now Patsy Cline and Tim McGraw's voices crooned about love and lust. Non smoking was the norm in public places, but occasionally Ned, the owner, declared it a special week-end and turned the smoke-eater back on, stocked his out-dated cigarette machine with Marlboros so the customers coughed and inhaled as they spent their money.

Daisy had dressed in a sleeveless and low cut black shirt which she had tucked into black ankle pants. She teetered on high heeled wedgies. Her silver hoop earrings, bracelets, and sleek blonde hair shimmered in the gloomy interior of the bar.

Roma had looked around, completely surprised at the crowd and the carnival atmosphere of the place. She was wearing stark white slacks and a white shirt. She sparkled, wearing all her gold, the dangling gold earrings and all the rest of her jewelry was displayed on her lusty shape. She'd pulled all her red hair into a pony tail but had left tendrils that brushed her cheeks. Her make-up was probably a little heavier than the locals were used to, but they'd heard she was from another country and blamed it on that.

By now the town had heard about the playful stunt her jealous boy-friend had done by slipping a snake in her suitcase, and the hunt for it in Daisy's house. And now just this morning, Hecter, the refuse collector, had declared finding a full suitcase of good clothes in Daisy's garbage.

What in the world was that about, they wondered?

The bartender, a good looking woman came over. "Hello Daisy, what can I bring you and your friend to drink?" she asked.

"Let's have some wine, what do you think?" Daisy asked Roma, who nodded.

And after a few minutes they were surrounded by the town folk who waited to meet the new visitor. And not too far down the bar, Daisy noticed that rich, handsome Reed Conners was there with her second cousin, Lindy Lewis. That notorious woman whom she'd heard had burned her big mansion down there in Minneapolis, and probably had killed her husband too, they said.

-8-

Daisy gave her second cousin Lindy Lewis a quick once over as they sat at the bar, and although she was a few years older, Daisy had to admit Lindy still had a youthful look about her. Of course, she had never had any kids to wear her out and that husband she'd snared had been said to be a prize, Daisy had heard through relatives.

It was Saturday afternoon of the Labor Day holiday and Daisy and Roma were downtown in Birch Lake at the Legion club. The two men who had given up their seats for them at the bar had promptly moved in.

"Daisy, you didn't tell me you had such handsome guys in your town!" Roma said as she took an offer of a cigarette from one of them and then blew smoke toward the ceiling after the other had lit it for her.

"Oh, sure and you've only met a few. This is Ed, he owns the car business," Daisy said, turning to the well built man dressed in a suit and tie. "And meet Stan, he owns the Woodsmen café." The two men crowded around Roma and Daisy.

"How long are you going to stay Roma?" Ed asked. "I see you drive a Lexus. Are you leasing?"

Roma studied him for a minute. "Cripes, you certainly ask a lot of questions.

"Well, there's a lot I want to know about you, like what kind of car I can sell you." He moved closer to her.

Roma sat back. "Wow, Daisy how did you let this charmer get away?"

Daisy laughed. "Now girlfriend, don't settle on the first one you meet. My town is full of exciting guys."

"And there's me," Stan said. "And I'll give you freebies any time in my place."

"And you've got to really watch out for this one," Daisy smiled, nudging Stan. "Before you know it, you'll have gained a hundred pounds. He's a great cook!"

The noise level increased as the afternoon wore on, as more people found their way to the Legion. Daisy and Roma were popular as the male presence far outnumbered the unescorted females. Daisy had always seemed mysterious and elusive since coming back to her homeland. And now that a new female had come to town, word had spread like wildfire and the single and not so single angled up to make their acquaintance.

"I'm taking my boat out," Ed said then, "and I'd like to invite you ladies out for a cruise this evening."

Roma's eyes lit up. "What do you think Daisy, should we go?"

"It's been a long time since I was out on the water. Sure let's go." Daisy said.

"I've got appetizers being delivered at five," Ed checked his watch and downed his drink. "Daisy, you know where I'm docked. I've got some other people coming on too, so I've got to take off and meet them there." And Ed and Stan finished their drinks and hurried out of the Legion.

The music still echoed and bounced off the walls and the smoke eater struggled to whisk the noxious fumes outside. As Daisy and Roma had finished their cocktails and stood to go, Daisy stumbled slightly on her high-heeled wedgies and Roma steadied her friend.

"I'll drive," she said to Daisy and held out her hand, "Where's your keys?"

"Silly," Daisy said with a crooked smile, "It's just two blocks to the boat landing so we can walk."

"Okay," Roma said as they left the Legion.

"Lord," Daisy said as they got outside on the street, "I don't need to smoke for a long time."

"Me either," Roma replied and blew out a breath. "Okay, I can smell the water. Show me the way!"

The one main street in Birch Lake was tangled with traffic on this weekend as the townspeople crowded into downtown to see the action. An antique car show would go on and now the shiny, renovated autos of the 60's and 70's were making their way into town.

"Cripes, I remember some of those cars," Roma said as they walked down the street. "

"Well, I do too, but I love my Porsche. It cost a bundle but it's so worth it."

They walked down the street and passed by the real estate office, the well-drilling company and then the big car lot that took up half the block and then Ed's office. And even though its owner was out partying, music poured out from its speakers and his salesmen were busy bustling around the new shiny vehicles. The last business on the way and set back from the street was a new company called Gulbrenson's.

"This is a funeral place," Daisy whispered as they both hurried along, "I get chills every time I go by."

"Why?" Roma asked. "We need these people, and think about it, we all like to look nice, even when we croak."

This made Daisy giggle. "I've met the man who owns it," she said then. "He seems okay, but some of the people here shy away from him."

Now the scene changed as they came to the lake shore. About a dozen docks extended out over the water to which boats, large and small were anchored.

"There's Ed's, we call it the floating palace," Daisy said now and Roma followed as they stepped out onto the dock. Music blared from the boat and people stood ready to cross the gangplank onto the finery. The boat was a thirty eight foot Formula and Daisy had heard it was a showpiece.

Ed was there now and stood ready to help his guest's board. When Daisy's turn came he gave her a hug and the same with Roma.

"Go below and get a cocktail," he said, "Stan is down there." He had banished his usual suit and tie and now wore a Tommy Bahama red flowered shirt and shorts. The red accentuated his tan face and blond hair.

The women went below as he directed where Stan was behind a bar shaking a martini. A couple stood waiting for their drinks and Daisy saw it was the owner of the funeral home with an escort.

She sucked in her breath. What she hadn't told Roma was that the times she had run into him around town previously, she would get some creepy vibes. But she attributed it to the business he was in.

She nudged Roma over closer and said, "Tom, I'd like you to meet my friend Roma. She is here visiting from Norway."

Tom shook hands with Roma, and then turned to introduce his partner. "Daisy and Roma, this is Athena." And they shook hands. He continued, "Athena surprised me yesterday with a visit too."

Then Roma turned and hurried back up the short stairway to the deck. Daisy followed her. "For God's sake Roma, what is the matter?"

"I've got to get the hell off this boat. Daisy, that woman! I've seen her before!"

"Who? Do you mean Athena?" Daisy whispered as they stood close aboveboard.

Roma's hair tumbled around her face, loosened by the wind. She clutched Daisy's hand. "I've seen her before, in Norway. That woman is a friend of Gunther!"

Daisy gaped at her friend. "No--, that's not possible!

"Anything is possible!" Roma's voice was hoarse now. "I don't put anything past him."

"I just can't believe all this," Daisy protested.

"You don't know Gunther Muller. He most likely had me checked out even before we got together that first night. And, of course that would mean he checked you out too!"

"Roma, you didn't tell him anything about your ex-husband, did you?"

"Are you nuts, I don't tell anyone about him and what he did!

-9-

Roma gaped at Daisy's question, and then continued, "I've found that as soon as people find out who I am, they remember those news articles about him and they want money."

"I suppose so, although it wouldn't hurt if he gave some away. After all what is your husband going to do with it all anyway? Millions!"

"Ex-husband, Daisy." Roma hissed.

"Oh yes, sorry. Did he ever give any to your kids?"

"Finally, but they had to get an attorney and sue his ass. You know I got half of the millions in my divorce, didn't you?"

"No, but good for you Roma. Can I ask how much?"

Roma laughed at her good friend. "Of course you can," she whispered, "listen to this I got exactly twenty million from the asshole."

"You mean he got all those millions just for inventing that thing that computer company bought?" Daisy asked with an incredulous look on her face.

They were still standing on the deck of Ed's boat out on Birch Lake. He had invited them to join a group for an evening on his big luxurious floating palace. The women had accepted his invitation and joined the party. They had gone down below for drinks when Roma had turned around abruptly after being introduced to Tom and his friend Athena and immediately ran back up the steps to the deck with Daisy following. She whispered, "I know her, I've been followed after all!"

Daisy took her arm. "Roma, listen. Don't say anything more. We haven't gone too far out yet so I'll find Ed and tell him we need to go back to Birch right away!"

Roma nervously pinned her windblown hair up and off her face. "I know for sure I've seen that woman before, Daisy," Roma whispered!"

"Maybe Athena has a sister or a twin, Roma," Daisy said. "You know they say everyone has a double."

"For Christ sake, who said that? Who are they?" Roma's anxious voice shook. "Roma, sit down here and don't move, and I'll find Ed."

Daisy disappeared through the party-goers who were well on their way to a liquor induced time. Music by the Beach Boys blared louder now from the speakers as the sun began its decline in the west over the water. Almost immediately Roma felt the evening breeze on her face as the boat turned around and sped toward shore. Daisy hurried back to her side.

"Okay, we'll be back in the harbor in a minute, Roma and we'll go back to my place. I just told Ed you were sick." Daisy sat down with Roma on a bench seat and soon they were back to town. Ed brought the boat smoothly to the dock and Stan helped them over the gangplank.

"So sorry we have to leave," Roma lied to him, "I've lived on the water all my life in Norway when I was a kid, but now for some reason today I've gotten sea sick."

"If you feel better later call me on my cell and we'll come back for you." Ed said and planted a kiss on her cheek.

"Thanks, for everything," Daisy said to Ed. They stepped onto the dock and started walking through town. "Now for God's sake Roma, tell me more about this person, you must be mistaken."

"Cripes, I'm sure, Daisy," Roma whispered as the two women hurried to Daisy's house.

Dropping their purses on a table and sliding out of their high-heels inside the foyer, they went to the kitchen.

"We need to eat, how about a ham sandwich?" Daisy asked. "Roma, sit at the counter while I rustle up some food."

As Daisy busied herself around the kitchen Roma began to talk. "Daisy," she said, "what I didn't tell you was, one night I went to a party with Gunther, and it was one of the very few times we ever went out in public. While there he got a phone call and he told me to grab a cab and that he would meet me in two hours at my house. So I was somewhat miffed that he had to leave and I had a few cosmos too many."

Roma stopped talking and took a bite of the sandwich Daisy had finished making and put on the counter top. "Yumm- this is good," she murmured and swallowed. "Well, anyway to make a long story short, I got friendly with another woman there, and we exchanged sob stories about our lives. Mostly I did when I think about it, And Daisy, I blabbed to her about my millions and also my ex's inventions. By the way, listen to this. My boys told me their dad has another weird thing he's working on!"

Daisy had been busy cleaning up the cupboard after making the sandwiches and now poured them each a glass of milk, and took a seat at the counter too.

"Go back Roma. Tell me about this woman. Did she recognize you today?"

"Hell, I was so stunned, I don't remember."

"Well, even if she did, what's the difference?" Daisy took a bite of her sandwich.

"Don't you see Daisy; this was a very elite group of people at that party. Gunther wouldn't have gone there otherwise. I think they were all in the same business, killers for hire!" Roma slapped a hand on the countertop for emphasis

"No--," Daisy ventured, "I'd think anyone in that business would be very private."

"Daisy, listen I know as soon as Gunther found I had vanished, he would have interrogated her and all my acquaintances. And now, for Christ's sake, she has come here to kill me!"

Daisy was a little tired of all the drama but she loved her old friend. Twenty years ago, they had met in a suburb in Minneapolis and lived next door to each other. Roma had fallen in love and married just after coming to the US from Norway. Then they had husbands who worked downtown and they were both stay- at- home moms with growing kids. It was in the days of living on a tight budget to pay the mortgage and exchanging recipes to stretch the menus.

She shook her head now and said, "Roma, listen to me! Why?"

"Simple! Daisy, he's a killer! He did tell me once that he'd had his eye on me even before we met. No one leaves me, he said once!"

Daisy could only stare at her.

"That same person told me that two of his former lovers disappeared mysteriously years ago." Roma said.

"Oh for God's sake Roma, do you know for sure?"

Roma nodded her head and went on, "I know the fucker must have arranged our meeting, because he wants my millions too. That's the real reason he said I couldn't break off our relationship. And I'll bet that woman who calls herself Athena is a killer too and she is here to do it!"

The two women were so intense on their conversation they didn't see the red racer scoot across the wooden floor in the kitchen on its way back to its home in the yarn basket in the lanai.

-10-

Daisy and Roma sat in Daisy's kitchen in Birch Lake eating ham sandwiches and gulping ice cold milk. The sun had set and a breeze had come up around the countryside causing the last remaining leaves on the trees to dance and drift through the air. They had spent the afternoon in the Legion bar downtown drinking rum and cokes and without any dinner, they were starving. They were talking about Roma's sobering discovery that the woman posing as Athena was the same person she had met at a party in Norway weeks ago.

"Gunther has no doubt offered a bonus to whoever could take me out first!" Roma's voice was barely above a whisper.

Daisy was silent and let Roma rave on, and then she finally said, "Okay, let's go out on the lanai and have one last smoke, and you've got to try to relax. How about this, we go and see Sheriff Monte tomorrow and talk to him."

Roma gawked at her. "Do you really think he could stop something like this?"

"I'm not sure but we have to tell him so he can be on the alert."

"I suppose you're right." Roma said and followed Daisy out to the lanai. Here the breeze from the lake whisked through the room and the moon flickered over the waves that hummed toward shore. Daisy turned on the outside lights which lit up the landscaped backyard. Pots of blooming lilies edged the blue-green water of the pool and a group of padded chaises and tables stood off to one side. The manicured lawn dropped gracefully down to the lake.

"Oh wow, this is beautiful!" Roma took a seat and put her feet up on a hassock.

Daisy sat on a chair and shared the hassock with her. "That's right; you haven't been here since I had all this work done."

"I'm surprised to see all this opulence right here in this small town, Daisy."

Daisy laughed, "I love the lake but I don't like to swim in it. This is the only pool in town."

"I'd like to try it out." Roma said.

"The pool? Sure, it's supposed be nice tomorrow."

Roma's feet hit the floor. "I mean now!"

"Now?" It's late!" Daisy echoed.

"Daisy, I need to get some exercise. I've been cooped up for days traveling." And she took her shirt off and started to unzip her trousers.

Daisy laughed, "Okay, wait for me, I'll get some suits!"

"Suits! Hell, we don't need them," and Roma stood there without a stitch on.

Peals of laughter echoed in Daisy's house then as they took a minute and compared their enhanced bustlines and their bikini wax lines. Then Daisy turned off the outside spotlights and they ran to the pool and jumped in.

Roma was a league swimmer and did laps back and forth in the cool clear water. Daisy did one over to the chairs and pulled herself out. Swiping her hair off her face, she grabbed a towel and wrapped it around herself and sat down to watch.

It was going on midnight and she was tired. It had been a long day yesterday when Roma had arrived and then they'd had the snake hunt, and they'd drank a couple bottles of wine. Today they spent the afternoon at the Legion and then out on Ed's boat. Maybe they'd sleep in tomorrow but they had one more day of the holiday to celebrate. There was the flea market and craft show and then the parade at 2 0'clock to go to.

"Hey girlfriend," Roma's voice brought her back to the moment. "Watch this," and she climbed up to the diving board and posed beautifully and then slid almost silently into the water. Surfacing she swam to the ladder and came out of the water.

"Wow, you're good!" Daisy said handing her a towel. "You can rinse off the chlorine in the shower over there," and she pointed to an enclosure that leaned against the house.

Coming back after the shower, Roma fell into a chair. "Cripes, I needed that but now I'm done! They can come and get me and I don't care!" She said knotting the beach towel on her chest.

"Should we call it a day?" Daisy asked.

"Oh cripes yes!" Roma whispered.

It was close to noon when they met in the kitchen the next day. It was Monday and the holiday was still going strong in Birch Lake. Roma was wearing Daisy's red robe again and as she perched on a stool she said to Daisy, "I know Gunther knows I'm here."

Daisy handed her a cup of coffee and said, "Let's try not to worry, Roma. I've got cinnamon rolls baking in the oven."

Roma went on, "You're right. Tomorrow, I've got to go somewhere and buy some clothes and a cell phone. Do you have a dress shop anywhere around here?"

Daisy smiled. "You've got to go a ways but there's a Chico's and a Loft in Rayburn. That's about fifty miles from here."

"I have the rest of my things packed and ready to be shipped here back in Norway, but I have to notify the company when I've found a house."

"Too bad, you threw all your things away." Then Daisy smiled, "I wonder if you will see your stuff on anyone around town!"

"I shudder to think about it," Roma said. "I do remember when I opened my suitcase I saw this snake crawl right out of its skin."

"It must have shed it." Daisy exclaimed, not knowing the red racer was curled up for warmth under the edge of the cupboard right next to the oven. She shivered, and then changed the subject. "Here, have some coffee and the cinnamon rolls in the oven are just about done." As they sat enjoying their morning, Daisy's phone rang,

"Good morning," she said.

"And good morning to you Daisy," a woman's voice greeted her. "This is Athena. I met you yesterday on that boat."

Taken aback, Daisy hesitated as she went on.

"I'm sorry you and your friend had to leave so early, and we didn't get a chance to visit." Athena's voice was smooth but held a slight Scandinavian accent.

"Yes, so sorry, but she's better today." Daisy answered.

"Wonderful," Athena purred, "then I would like to invite you and Roma over here to my friend's house tonight for an early supper after the parade. Tom will be joining us for brandy later."

While this woman was talking, Daisy was trying to whisper to Roma who was on the line. Roma's eyes bugged when she heard it was Athena on the other end.

"Thank you, we'd love to come." Daisy said, "Can we bring anything?" This was custom in this small town to ask after accepting an invitation.

"Oh no," Athena said, "5'oclock then?"

Daisy hung up the phone and looked apprehensively at Roma.

"See there," Roma's face paled and she whispered, "She's going to kill me!"

"No, not right here." Daisy protested recalling the safety and protectiveness of belonging she felt in her town. "She can't do it right here."

Roma put her head in her hands and was silent. Daisy poured more coffee for each of them and then stood up from her stool.

"Roma, I'm sorry. I should have refused her invitation, but I didn't know what to say at the moment. Should I call back and say we have another engagement?"

Roma raised her head. "It won't make any difference. She's one of Gunther's crowd."

"Are you sure Roma?" Daisy asked.

"I never forget a face. She's the woman I got drunk with and told her things I don't even remember." Roma took a long drink of her coffee.

"Did you mention me?"

"Oh, we talked about girlfriends." Roma put a hand over her mouth. "You know, they lost me at the airport there in Oslo, but here's what they did. The fucker knew eventually I'd end up here and he sent her here to pose as a friend of a resident."

"But they wouldn't dare just kill you here. Everyone would know!" Daisy protested.

"Daisy, it's perfect. Don't you get it? Tom has a funeral business and no doubt does cremations. How hard would that be to kill and cremate me, then dig a hole in this big forest here and bury my ashes?"

"Oh my God, Roma, that couldn't happen!"

"Well, believe me, it could easily! My bed-partner is a killer. Remember he said he would kill me if I ever left him!"

Daisy got off the kitchen stool and reached her telephone book in a drawer. "Roma, I've got an idea, I know a man who lives here who could help. He's a retired attorney and also an investigator for a firm in Minneapolis."

"What good would that do?" Roma asked.

"I don't know," Daisy answered, "but we can't just sit here like pigeons, we've got to do something!

"I need to get myself a gun!" Roma exclaimed.

"Oh, for God's sake! Roma listen, his name is Reed Conners and he lives right here in Birch." Then she reached down to open the oven door and take out the perfectly browned and heavenly tasting cinnamon rolls.

-11-

"Who is Reed Conners?" Roma asked as she sat in Daisy's kitchen. It was the final day of the three day Labor Day weekend. She had been in Birch Lake for several days and talked again of her fear that her old boyfriend, was out to kill her. She added, "Daisy, what the hell could Conners do anyway?"

Daisy wiped the countertop and poured more coffee. She gotten up early to put a pan of cinnamon rolls in the oven and the aroma filled the kitchen.

"Actually I don't know," She murmured. "But he is an investigator and a lawyer. It wouldn't hurt to talk to him. Tell him about this."

Roma shook her head, and then said, "I think I will just get a gun!"

"Do you know how to use one?" Daisy asked.

"Hell yes. My dad took me and my brothers to the range every week growing up. We hunted for our supper sometimes."

"You mean for wild game?" Daisy looked at her friend, "you never told me that!"

Roma gave a short laugh. "We were poor and we hunted in the forests near Oslo for everything; rabbits, deer, and birds."

"Roma, you never talked much about your childhood all those years when we lived by each other in Minneapolis."

"Well, remember we were busy with our families, and our husbands."

They were both silent as the memory of those long gone days came to mind. Then Daisy said, "For God's sake, that's over and here we are; kids grown, single and independent!"

They laughed and raised their coffee cups in a salute. "Okay I'm going to look up Reed's phone number and give him a call." When he didn't answer, she left a message for him to return the call. "Let's get ready to go uptown. The parade starts at two and after that we can go to the car show."

"That's where the men are, right?" Roma laughed.

"I was going to mention that too." Daisy went over to the cooled cinnamon rolls and slid them out onto a plate.

"Cripes Daisy, my rolls never look this good." Roma said and took a bite.

"Thanks Roma. But let's hurry and get ready. Do you need something of mine to wear today?"

"Have you got a shirt or a top of some kind? I can wear my jeans again."

They finally got to the festivities and enjoyed the day, then after stopping at home to freshen up they were on their way to Athena's and Tom's house for dinner.

Opening the door at their first ring of the bell, Athena stood clad in a slim pencil style long black skirt and a see through white fluff of a top which showed off a lacy slip underneath. Her long black hair was tightly wound into a knot on top of her head. Her make-up was done beautifully.

"Hello," she said and stood aside for Daisy and Roma to enter. "I am so glad you both could come."

"Thank you for inviting us," Daisy said stepping into the foyer and putting her purse on a table. "What do you think of our town? Or have you been here before Athena?"

"No, this is my first time. My friend loves it and wanted me to see and meet his townspeople. Come in please."

Roma had stood silently and now walked in with Daisy, discreetly studying Athena and her actions. When she had met and talked to this woman at the party in Oslo, she had called herself Maida, and there, she had appeared very masculine wearing denims and no make-up.

Could she be mistaken, thinking Athena was the same person as Maida, a killer for hire just like her ex-boyfriend Gunther?

She repeated Daisy's thanks and smiled now at her hostess then remarked, "I didn't hear where you are from Athena?"

They had now moved into the huge living room and Athena showed them to a pair of red suede couches that sat near a fireplace. The room was beautifully designed in beige and red accents with woven rugs covering the gleaming wood floors.

"Please have a seat," she invited. Daisy and Roma sat side by side on one couch. A liquor cart stood nearby the other.

"Now, I have a lovely bottle of wine from the Silverado winery. May I pour you ladies some?" Athena asked standing ready.

She was the picture of a calm experienced hostess, but Roma wasn't fooled for one minute. She smiled at Athena as she was handed the crystal glass of Pinot Noir, but apparently the woman was avoiding her question. "I love this kind of champagne," she said now to appear sociable.

"Your friend has a lovely home," Daisy remarked, "have you known Tom long?"

"Sure, we've been acquaintances for ages." Athena sat down and took a delicate sip from her glass.

Roma took a sip of her wine too, but a small one. For all she knew this woman could be poisoning them. She noticed that apparently Daisy was downing hers without worrying about it.

As they made small conversation, Roma saw this woman had the same mannerisms as the woman who called herself Maida in Norway just months ago. Her eye color had been blue then, but now Roma saw her eyes were green. Well, that was easy to change with contacts! Good lord, she had to do something and not sit there like a dummy. Hell, she was not going down without a fight.

"Are we too early? Who else is coming?' She asked now, curiously.

"You and Daisy are my only guests tonight. I wanted it to be a cozy party just for us."

Roma thought about that for a minute. "Have you traveled much?" she asked Athena again and this time made direct eye contact with the woman.

"Some," Athena said but again immediately changed the subject. Roma nudged Daisy with an elbow at that, trying to convey a message of Athena's vague answers.

"I enjoyed the parade," Athena commented. "There were so many homemade floats and high school bands."

"Have you ever seen anything like a small-town parade before?" Roma asked still fishing for clues.

Athena hesitated and then went on. "No, I'm guilty, this is new to me. But I loved every minute of it!" She smiled at them.

Roma blew out a quiet breath. For sure, this person had to be the same woman as the one in Norway. The same woman whom she had gotten quite inebriated with, and among other things confided that she knew what Gunther did for a living. Now she saw the picture clearly. When she exclaimed she was leaving him because he was a killer for hire, he threatened, and said 'no one leaves me"! She was sure after he found out she was gone, he sent his goons to watch the airlines.

But she thought she had found that out in time at the airport back in Norway when that suspicious looking man had been arrested. But apparently Maida/Athena had been there following her too and gotten on the same plane? And if the two women were one and the same, where had Athena been since then? Roma had been sure no one had followed her when she hid out at that shelter.

Hell, this was giving her a headache! All the time this was parading through her head, she was trying to look interested in the conversation going on between Athena and Daisy and entered now asking, "Is that your home?" When Athena mentioned the city of Hamburg located in Germany.

"Jesus no. I was just traveling through a number of years ago." She said and ran a manicured hand over her already well coifed hair. Getting up from her seat after checking Daisy's glass she asked now, "May I refill your wine?" To which Daisy held up her glass.

"Roma, you're not drinking yours, don't you like it?" Athena asked.

Daisy came to her defense and answered for her. "Her stomach has been acting strangely all day." Then she looked pointedly at her and said, "Just take small sips Roma."

Roma stood up suddenly putting a hand over her mouth. "Athena, may I use your restroom?"

"Why yes, yes by all means. I'll show you the guest bath." And Roma dutifully followed Athena off to the central part of the house. Coming to a closed door, Athena opened it for Roma and stood aside. Just take your time, and call if you need help."

To which Roma waited for a few minutes then peeked out the door and saw the coast was clear. Then she tiptoed out and looked quickly in the many doors until she found what looked like Athena's room. Slipping in, she furiously searched for something, something that would give her a clue as to who this woman was.

Bingo! She found it in a coat pocket. A crumpled canceled luggage check issued to a customer to claim luggage arriving from Oslo, Norway. The date the

same day as when she had arrived! Roma almost
threw up for real. Sucking in a breath, she had to get
Daisy and get the hell out of there.

Coming out of the bathroom, her face did really
look pale and she said, "Daisy, I need to get to a
hospital. I'm terribly sick!" And as they rushed from
Athena's dinner party, Roma hissed, "We need to find
Reed Conners right away. She's the killer!"

-12-

It was only six blocks from Tom Gulburnson's home to Daisy's and her and Roma's high heels clicked and clattered on the concrete sidewalks as they hurried away from the funeral home where they had been invited to dinner by Athena, a friend of his. The last hours of the long holiday Labor Day weekend were coming to a close as tourists and weekend residents were packing up and going home. For some there was a sigh of relief that all the commotion was done with and for others a sigh as loneliness again claimed its occupants.

"Roma slow down, don't run," Daisy whispered as soon as they had gotten out the door. "People going by in cars will stop to see what's wrong."

"Jesus, we should have driven over here!" Roma huffed.

"I know, but it was a nice night so I though the walk would be good for us." A cool breeze had whipped in from the lake in just the short time they had been having wine with Athena.

"We didn't even bring jackets, Daisy." Roma complained and rolled down the sleeves of the shirt she had borrowed. She hunched her shoulders as they hurried along.

Daisy frowned at her friends complaints, but went on, "I can't believe that friend of Tom's is a killer, Roma. Are you sure?" Her silver blonde hair had straightened from the humidity and its tousled look now hung in pixie wisps around her face. She had worn a white terry cloth outfit with long sleeves and pants so she was not shivering.

"Yes, I'm sure. That luggage claim ticket I found in one of her pockets was it! It was for the same day and same airlines that I was on, Daisy!"

"For God's sake, then she must be. But you'd never know by looking at her."

"Gunther didn't look like a cold blooded killer either," Roma whispered, "He looked like a well dressed business man."

Daisy whispered back, "I can't believe this is happening. I'll give Reed Conners a call again and maybe we can even see him tonight!"

"Daisy, weren't you surprised that Athena hadn't invited other people over tonight too?"

"Actually I did wonder about it."

Roma blew out a breath. "When she said we were the only ones that was when I started to really suspect something sinister going on."

After a few minutes they were at Daisy's door. The lights blazed in the kitchen as they came in the back door and the faint aroma of cinnamon and coffee still hung in the air.

"Damn, I must have left the lights on," she exclaimed curiously.

"Daisy, did Conners call?" Roma asked impatiently.

"No, no," Daisy picked up the telephone which stood on the cupboard and dialed.

Reed answered now and after some pleasantries, Daisy asked, "Reed, do you have some time available? You met my friend Roma earlier and she needs some advice. I suggested you might be able to help her."

She heard him murmur to someone in the background. "Sure Daisy, I'll do what I can. Do you want to bring her over or should I come to your house?"

"We can come over, if that's okay. It's not too late tonight is it?" Daisy asked.

"We just got home from Ed's party. It went on all evening. Hey, I saw you and your friend leave early," Reed commented.

"We did, that's when this started with Roma. Listen, thanks for making time for us tonight."

"No problem, bring your friend over and I'll see what I can do." Reed said.

Roma looked at Daisy expectantly after she hung up the phone. "What time?" she asked.

"We can go now," Daisy said and they grabbed jackets.

Leaving Birch Lake, and a few miles out of town they turned off highway #371 onto Reed's private road that led through woods and right down to his home on the other side of the lake. His yard was ablaze from floodlights and they saw his birch trees were staging their last hurrah of colors with their leaves and their white trunks.

"This is beautiful," Roma murmured as they parked beside a gleaming, silver Lexus. "I hope we're not interrupting, it looks like he must have company."

"Well, he didn't mention anybody visiting." Daisy said and before they got to his door, Reed stepped out and greeted them.

"Hey ladies, come on in." And he held the door open and ushered them into a foyer, and then into his living room. A fire burned in the fireplace sending a faint apple scent through the room and low jazz was playing. Lamps were turned down low and the wood floor, maroon leather furniture and book cases warmed the room. Lindy Lewis, Daisy's cousin was curled up on the couch

"I'd like you to meet Roma Hurst, a friend," Daisy said to them and the three women smiled politely at each other. Daisy and Roma sat down in the easy chairs. Reed ran a hand over his forehead and brushed his hair back.

"What can I get you to drink?" He offered. "Wine or a beer?"

Both Daisy and Roma murmured their thanks and said they would love some ice water if possible. And after getting settled, Reed asked, "Now, what can I help you with?"

"Roma, tell Reed," Daisy nodded for Roma to began.

Roma swallowed. It wasn't often she got nervous and frightened, but this had scared her. She did not like not being in control! Now her face flushed and her lips trembled as she said, "Mr. Conners, I have a hired killer after me! I'm from Oslo, Norway and she has followed me here. We met her tonight!"

Reed took a drink of his beer. "Roma, I guess you better start at the beginning. And call me Reed."

Roma sipped her water, then set her glass down and straightened her shirt sleeves as she tried to settle her nerves.

"I've been seeing a man over there for months. His name is Gunther Muller, but of course that's not his real name, I'm sure. I've stayed with him at length, now and then. I heard rumors that he was a killer for hire and found that they were true. When I told him I knew this about him and was leaving, he threatened. He's had me watched and apparently I was even followed from the airport there to over here." Roma took a breath and tucked her pony-tail in tighter.

"How can you be sure, Roma?" Reed asked.

"Let me assure you, I am sure. I saw and met this same woman tonight. You see I recognized her when I was introduced to her out on Al's boat today. That's why we left!"

"You knew her in Oslo? How did you find out he was a killer for hire? That's always guarded information."

"It was a gathering that Gunther invited me to attend with him. He never took me out anywhere in public but at this one, he got a call and hurried out and left me there alone with these strangers. He told me to grab a taxi to get home. Well, I got pissed and drank too much, and then talked too much." Roma's face paled at this.

"Are you saying you talked too much to this woman? What did you say?" Reed asked.

"That I knew Gunther was a killer for hire. And also, that I had gotten millions in a settlement."

"Then what?" Reed asked again.

Roma whispered. "When I told him I was leaving, he threatened and said, 'he'd kill me if I tried! That no one leaves him unless he said so!'"

"What's the connection to that woman here?" Reed wanted to know.

"Athena, the woman that was with Tom Gulbranson, is that woman!" Roma whispered. "I suspected who she was when I met her out on the boat today. Then she invited us over to Tom's house for dinner this evening, and Reed, I found out for real that she is after me!"

"How? Do I want to know this?" Reed ran a hand through his hair.

"Reed listen, I found a baggage claim ticket that proved she had been on the same plane from Oslo as I was on!" Roma exclaimed and pulled it out of her shirt pocket.

"You didn't," he exclaimed but reached for it. After studying it he commented, "Roma, this only says someone had something to pick up at the airlines baggage department on that date. It doesn't prove someone was out to kill you! Honestly, what do you think I should do?"

"Well, first of all you've got to get me a gun, a "clean piece". I don't want it to be traceable and I'll pay. Reed, I don't plan on going down for this fucker!"

Lindy sat up and chimed in, "Good for you Roma. Get the scum-bag!"

Lyn Miller LaCoursiere

-13-

Roma smiled at Lindy's remark. "That's exactly what I want to do. I don't intend to willingly give up my life for this ass-hole!" Then she added hotly, "I can't believe I slept with the mother-fucker!"

Reed listened intently then remarked, "I don't sell firearms Roma, but I can recommend reliable sources for you to contact."

Judging by his remarks, Roma just didn't feel he understood her real situation.

"Reed," she said finally, "I repeat, I'm sure Gunther knew my whole history when I met him that first night. I'm sure all he had done was go to the internet and read about my divorce, and the whole dirty mess. About how my ex made millions on his invention and how I, the cheating wife, took most of it."

"Why would he have wanted to look you up, Roma?" Reed asked then.

Roma tightened her lips in disapproval. "When I moved back to Norway after my divorce, the Oslo papers did a story on me and how I was bringing my millions home to line their coffers."

"This is where you're from then. How long had you been gone?"

"Twenty three years. I married a man in the US and raised a family here."

"Do you have this man's social security number and address? Also, I need to know who your informant was!"

Roma gave him Gunther Muller's address, but she didn't know his Social Security number. "And Reed," she said then, "I can't give you my informant's number. She'd be in danger if it got out she talked."

"Roma," Daisy nodded impatiently, "You've got to tell him all you know. How do you expect him to help if you're holding back important information?"

Roma stood up and walked around the room, then went to a window and looked out at the lake. She nervously picked at her lip.

"Okay, you're right Reed," she said then coming back to the couch and sitting down. "Her name is Ragna Dahle and she is with the "Daghloge," the Oslo daily newspaper.

Reed jotted down the information on his laptop as they talked. "What can you tell me about this Athena? I've met her several times around town with Tom Gullbranson."

"I can't remember anything else." Roma said now feeling totally exhausted. "Can I call you if anything else of consequence comes to mind?"

"Sure Roma. And I need your cell phone number. Now here's what I can do for you right now. I can notify Sheriff Monte and the department. Which means, they can do drive-bys past Daisy's house and also that they should be aware of strangers in town and their intentions."

Daisy stood up. "Okay, Reed thanks for your time. Nice to see you again Lindy"

Roma stood, and said to Reed, "Should we talk about your fee?"

"Let me look into this, Roma and I'll get back to you in a day or two."

"Thank you Reed," she said, "and I hope we didn't take up too much of your evening."

"Its fine, ladies," Reed said and then stood up. Lindy joined the group and then the exchange of smiles all around. "I'll be in touch," he said then holding the door for Daisy and Roma as they left his house.

"Well, that went well." Daisy exclaimed as they got in her Porsche. The fine engine purred as they spun out of his turn around driveway and back through the woods to the highway. "Don't you feel better now?" She asked Roma.

Roma tightened her full lips and purposely held her hands from picking at them. A habit she'd had for years when she was anxious.

"Yes, I feel better now, and I know he has to investigate, but what about now, tonight, tomorrow?"

"We'll just keep the doors locked and a good eye out for strangers. I'm not sure what to do about Athena though." Daisy said as they drove back to Birch Lake.

"I do. I'm going to that town you mentioned tomorrow to shop to replace the things I threw out, and I am going to buy a gun."

"Oh, for God's sake Roma. That's not a good idea."

"Oh yes, I'm not going to sit by and get killed."

"Well I know that, but with a gun in your hand you've got to be ready to kill too!"

Daisy exclaimed as she drove.

"Do I have a choice?" Roma said hotly. "What the hell would you do, Daisy?"

Daisy was silent. Then said, "I guess I don't know if I was up against the wall."

By now they were back in town and at Daisy's house. They drove in the garage and came into the house through a side entrance. And as soon as they came into the kitchen, Daisy realized there had been an intrusion. She stood still as the whiff of a stranger filled the air. She looked around.

"Roma" she whispered, "don't move, someone is in here, or has been!" Both women looked around warily as they stood quietly.

Living alone over the years, Daisy had witnessed several encounters with break-ins and intruders. And she had assumed an angry mantra in her fearful defense, which gave her the courage to even get out of bed in the middle of the night and march through rooms to investigate her premises. She tiptoed over and opened a drawer in the cupboard and took out the biggest flashlight she could buy, a shiny metallic blue. Now armed, she held up her hand for Roma to stay as she walked with a purposeful step through the kitchen door and into the living room.

But Roma stuck out her tongue and rolled her eyes at her and followed. They silently checked every room then and every closet, under beds and behind doors, but no one was there.

Coming back into the kitchen, Daisy put the flashlight down on the counter. The brilliantly colored tube stood a good 12 inches high.

Roma, still nervous said, "So that's our protection? We will certainly be killed!"

"For cripes sake Roma, calm down. Let's take a bottle of wine and go out to the lanai. We can smoke out there. Come on!"

"I might as well be drunk before I meet my maker," Roma grumbled.

And they sat in the moonlight lit room and smoked their cigarettes and enjoyed their wine. Nearby a lone figure quietly crept across the dock and slipped into the water. And the red racer awoke, restless and irritated now after being awakened from his nap in the basket of yarn. It tipped its head over the rim and silently slid to the floor.

"What time are you going shopping in the morning?" Daisy asked. She sat in one of the side rattan chairs and had her feet up on an ottoman and Roma had hers tucked under her, up on the couch.

Roma rolled her head on her shoulders, and then hunched her shoulders as she sat. "I'll leave early, Daisy, I don't know how long I will be there, but I'll check in with you."

"Do you know what to buy?"

"No, but the first thing I will do is find a personal shopper, and give her my sizes. Then I'll have lunch while she shops. "

"Don't you want to see what's out there?"

"Nope, Daisy, it's a waste of time to run around looking."

"Roma, remember how we used to shop together?"

"Sure Daisy, but that was then. We shopped for the best prices, now I've got money and I don't need to."

And as they discussed the merits of having money, the red racer lay just across the room behind a pot of ivy, its head up, feeling the vibrations of the voices in the air. But were they friends or foe?

-14-

After a full day celebrating the holiday with the afternoon parade, the car show and then the dinner invitation at Athena's and then meeting with Reed Conners, Daisy and Roma were both beat. Roma went to her new newly decorated guest bedroom, tossed her clothes on the foot of the bed, then blew out a breath as she stretched out under the comforter and instantly dosed off. But not into a blessed cocoon of sleep but into a game of frantic hide and seek. A game of being hunted. No real pictures came to her of who the hunters were; just that she was the prey.

After what seemed like this went on hour after hour, Roma awoke. She looked at her watch and saw it was just after 2 AM. The house and the town were still. Not a sound from racing traffic, or sirens, even horns from ocean traffic as she was used to in her own land, but just the whisper of an occasional breeze tickling leaves on one of the trees just outside the window in her bedroom.

She lay stock still and listened, then blinked in the dark. Something had awakened her tonight. Funny she hadn't had this trouble the first nights she had been here, she thought. She had slept soundly then.

Damn it, now she couldn't sleep. Wouldn't sleep until she knew what the hell had awakened her. She got out of bed and found the robe she had borrowed from Daisy. She tiptoed out of her darkened room and down the hallway into the kitchen. She stopped by the table, and then quickly ducked behind one of the tall-backed chairs. She stood stock still. Jesus, someone was there, right there in the kitchen and it wasn't Daisy. This was a much taller dark figure that stood in the corner of the room right next to the white refrigerator. It didn't move, but she could hear a soft fast rhythmic thumping. Then she realized it was her own heart beating out in fearful alarm. So loud, she was sure it could be heard by whoever was there in the same room.

The shade on the window over the sink was open but only a faint ray of moon-light lit up the room. Roma peered around the room through the dark looking for the light switch.

Now, is when she should have had a gun, for God's sake!

Could she get over to the cupboard drawer and find a butcher knife? But which drawer should she look in if she even got over there without getting killed. All these thoughts were flying through her head. Her red hair was standing up on her head and then spread down around her shoulders; hanging every which way. She tightened the belt on the long white robe around herself as she watched the still figure. It didn't dawn on her, that her appearance might be perceived as ghostlike as she had glided soundlessly into the kitchen.

Then to her fright, the dark silhouette let out a horrendous scream and fell over clutching a foot. "Help, help someone. Something bit me!" Roma heard the voice scream in the night.

She jerked out of her frozen stance and ran around the kitchen and finally found the damn light switch.

Just then Daisy burst in the room and gawked at the two people in her kitchen.

"What the hell is going on?" she yelled as she came to stand next to the person on the floor. "Roma, take that cell phone and call 911, right now," she ordered not wasting a minute.

"Who are you, how did you get in?" Daisy asked pissed. She stared at the individual dressed in a black sweat suit, with a black cap and a mask.

The person sprawled out on the floor and writhed in pain. Then wailed, "Help me, I need to get to a doctor."

"What bit you? What the hell are you talking about?" Daisy asked. Now she had her weapon, the big blue flashlight clasped in both her hands, ready.

The person gasped and sat up and held onto her ankle. "Please, I need help; I need to get to a doctor right away. Help me."

Daisy took a step closer to her. "Take off your mask," she ordered. When the person refused, she dashed over and snatched off her cap and ripped of the mask.

"What the hell, Athena?" The room was silent as the three women stared at each other. Roma had stood silently after calling for help and now she rushed over to Athena.

"You bitch, what were planning on doing? Stabbing me in my sleep?"

Then before anyone could say anything more, they all stared at the red racer as it slithered across the floor and in seconds disappeared out to the dark lanai.

Athena's eyes were huge in her pale face. She scrambled and tried to sit up, but fell back on the floor crying, "Oh no, it was supposed--. Call a doctor, I need an antidote right away or I will die!"

Daisy ran over and slammed the glass doors that closed off the lanai. "Before I do anything for you," she yelled down at Athena, "hand over your weapon.

Do you have a gun, a knife? I will not do a thing, I'll let you lay there and croak, you miserable excuse for a woman, if you don't."

Roma came over now. She put her hands on her hips and exclaimed, "How did you get in Daisy's house? And you've been in here before too, haven't you?" When Athena didn't answer, Roma kicked her bitten leg. "Bitch, you can lay there and die for all we care," Roma said harshly.

"Okay, okay," Athena whimpered and uncurled a hand.

Both Daisy and Roma came to stand closer by her and gawked at the shiny silver length of wire she had rolled up in her hand.

"You were going to choke me to death? That's a loupe isn't it?"

Athena moaned as she lay on the tiled kitchen floor. "I need help. Those retiles are poisonous."

"No kidding," Roma whispered and bent down now and poked a finger in her face. "And you put those two killers in my suitcase? Does Gunther know?"

Athena snickered in her misery. "He told me to do it!"

Daisy ran to the front door as the bell rang loudly. The young Deputy stood there. "Miz Daisy, I got here as soon as I could. What is wrong?" He straightened his stance with his hand ready on his gun. He can't be more than twenty years old, Daisy thought as she looked at him good for the first time. "I'm in charge. Sheriff Montes is gone," he exclaimed.

"Just bring your handcuffs and cuff this person and take her to the hospital," Daisy said leading him through the house to the kitchen. When they got there, Roma stood up and shook her head. "I think she's dead," she whispered.

With his hand on his gun, he hurried over, his belt jingled with all the tools he proudly carried. He kneeled at her side then and put a finger on her neck, tried again and then took a wrist. "I think you're right," he said then and stood up.

"I've got to call the doc." His voice shook. Damn, he had his first death on his hands and he needed to do it right.

Daisy and Roma backed away from the body, and then Daisy ran to a closet and found a blanket and covered her.

"I can't believe this," she said to Roma. "Now I have a dead woman on my kitchen floor and a killer snake loose in my lanai and it's only three o'clock in the morning. What's next?"

"I'm so sorry Daisy, I didn't mean for all this to follow me. When we get this straightened out with the sheriff department, I will stay at the motel up town until I can find a place of my own to buy."

"For God's sake Roma, don't even say that. You're my best friend!"

"Well, I don't want to wear out my welcome Daisy."

Daisy opened a cupboard and took out her cigarettes, "Come on, let's go out on the front porch and smoke." When she told the deputy where they were going he nodded. "I've got to stay with the body until the sheriff and the doc. gets here, but then I'll need to take a statement from both of you!" he remarked importantly.

Daisy had known him since he had been a skinny little red-haired kid and respected his proudly won employment. And now seeing his discomfort at just standing she said, "You can take a chair and sit while you wait."

When they came out the front door, some of the neighbors were clustered together peering at Daisy's house.

"Not another snake sighting, is there?" Someone called over.

"Too soon to tell," Daisy answered and waved a hand in dismissal as they sat.

"Sometimes small town living gets a little too small town for me." Daisy grimaced and murmured, then offered Roma her pack of Marlboros. They lit up.

Soon a white van that doc, the medical examiner drove, slid to a stop in her driveway and he climbed out, his build hampered by a cumbersome belly.

"Good morning Miss O'Dell," he addressed Daisy. "The deputy is inside?"

"Yes, he's in the kitchen with Athena." She took another drag of her cigarette. Good lord if anything else goes on --, she thought to herself.

And, it's a good thing she didn't know what else was in store for her!

-15-

Daisy and Roma had finished their cigarettes just as Deputy Gordie came out on the front porch. His usually pale complexion was blotchy with fiery red spots. They had awakened to find Athena, a hired killer, in Daisy's house. When she had been bitten by the red racer, the second killer snake that she was instrumental in planting in Roma's luggage, she had died almost instantly from her own devious efforts.

"Daisy, oh- I mean Miss Daisy," the Deputy said now, "I need to take you and your company into custody." He held handcuffs in one hand and his other hand clutched his gun handle.

"What?" Daisy exclaimed and then barked a short laugh. "Gordie," she said using his first name, "what are you talking about?"

Deputy sniffed and swiped a hand over his nose, the handcuffs jingling in the movement. "I'm taking you both in!"

"For what?" Roma echoed. Her voice loud and low.

"For what? A body is on your floor, dead. It could be a murder!"

"Oh for God's sake," Daisy broke in, "That woman lying on the floor broke into my home, a snake bit her, a snake that she was instrumental in getting into my home. She died from the snake bite! Her own fault."

"Are you kidding me? You can take our statements right here." Roma growled.

"You think we killed her?"

"Ma'am, like I said, I found a body. Now, if you both will proceed quietly to my cruiser, we can proceed to my department.

Daisy stood up straighter. "Deputy, where is Sheriff Monte?" She asked, out of patience.

Deputy Gordie sucked in his breath. "Sheriff Monte is away on business. I am in charge now!"

"Oh Jesus," Roma muttered to Daisy, "We're being sent to jail by a snot-nosed kid, carrying a gun. Daisy, do you think that thing is real?"

Daisy elbowed her to be quiet. "Deputy--," she said firmly, "I'm going to stay here until the doc has taken the body away. Now, why don't you sit down here and guard us so we don't get away." She indicated a wicker chair. The small group of neighbors had grown to what looked like a dozen, all standing in their various nightclothes, under a street light.

After a time, a shiny black hearse that belonged to Tom Gulbranson, the new funeral home owner, rolled up on her driveway.

"Oh Jesus, I hate the look of those death wagons." Roma whispered and Daisy shushed her again.

Deputy Gordie stepped outside and importantly to the driver's door. "Tom, we got a body in there. Doc is inside," he informed the man. Doc had been elected the county medical examiner years ago and Tom Gulbranson had been regarded as an all-around excellent addition to the community and just what they needed to give the busy doc a hand. But wouldn't he be surprised when he found he would be picking up the body of his own visitor.

"Tom, do not open the door to that sunroom. There is a poisonous snake loose in there. I will be outside here guarding these women," the Deputy said importantly, directing Daisy and Roma out of the house.

The time dragged on then as he paced, never taking his eyes off his prisoners.

"What the hell is taking them so long?" Roma complained to him. "Daisy, let's have another cigarette," and Daisy handed her the Marlboro pack.

By now it was going on early dawn, and a bird twittered in a nearby tree. Daisy's thoughts were going a mile a minute as she sat quietly. Her stomach growled nervously as a pickup pulled up to the cub and two strangers got out and swaggered to the porch. She saw they both wore uniforms and carried guns.

"Hey Gord, we heard Sheriff Montes is out of town and you got a murder on your hands. We came to help!"

"Yeah, good to have you," Deputy Gordie slapped them on their backs. "These here two females are my suspects. I found a dead woman in the kitchen."

The two men looked to be in their early twenties, and Daisy recognized them as deputies from another county.

My God, now they were really in trouble with three dime store cowboys with guns. And as time rolled along she saw things were steadily getting way out of hand as the three men stood off to the side, posturing and punching each other.

Roma was puffing on one cigarette after another. Just then the door burst open and Tom Gulbranson pushed his cart out with the body covered with a sheet. Doc followed. Both men were silent as they went to their vehicles and left.

Daisy and Roma stood up and turned to go in. "Hold on," the Deputy exclaimed holding a roll of yellow tape, "you can't go in there. This is a crime scene!"

"Well, you can call it whatever you want, but I am not leaving my home open for strangers to tramp through. There's a killer snake loose in there, but you can follow me in and watch while I lock up, and I will have the one and only key!" Daisy yelled to the three men who started for the door. She marched over and grabbed the door handle. Roma pushed her way over to her.

"And after I've locked up, I'm going to make a phone call." Daisy proclaimed. Deputy Gordie's hands were busy with one ready at his side in case he needed to use his gun and the roll of tape in the other. The two strangers clambered along behind.

"Jesus, at least we don't have to worry about her anymore," Roma whispered to Daisy as they came in the kitchen looking at where Athena had lain on the floor.

"Shush, don't say another word. Keep your eyes on the floor for that snake, just in case it got back in here!" Daisy whispered, grabbing up her cell phone. "Hurry, let's get out of here. I'm going to call Reed Conners."

Back outside, they stood together as Daisy dialed.

Reed answered on the second ring. "Reed," Daisy said, "I'm sorry to be calling you in the middle of the night, but we need you now, tonight. That woman Athena broke into my house, and another snake bit her and she died. The snake is still loose out in my lanai."

"She's dead?" Reed asked.

"Yes, the doc and Tom Gulbranson just left here with the body. Sheriff Montes is gone and we're in the hands of that young Deputy and a couple of his buddies from the next county. And he said we have to go with him down to the department."

"Goddamn, don't say a word Daisy. Go down to the precinct with him and I'll be there in a few minutes!"

"All right now, ladies," Deputy Gordie ordered, "come on now and don't do anything foolish," he ordered now as he held his hand ready on his gun handle. They all waited as Daisy locked the door and heard the click as it locked into place.

The Deputy handed the roll of yellow tape to the two strangers. "I need you guys to unroll this and run it around the house for me." They eagerly took the tape and disappeared around the side.

"Now ladies, I'm taking you in for questioning in the death of Athena Dahl." His face had a red mottled look as he flung the back door of his cruiser open.

"I can't believe this is happening!" Roma exclaimed seeing the wire mesh enclosure separating them, as she followed Daisy in to the vehicle. "Jesus, I'm going to jail!"

"We are not going to jail," Daisy whispered. "We are just going to tell what happened. We've got nothing to hide."

And then as the car started to move the deputy turned on the siren just as they burst out of the driveway and flew down the street.

Daisy put her hands over her ears and just shook her head. Roma hung onto the sides of the seat, and swore at this turn of events.

When they got downtown, a train of cars filled with curious citizens followed. Deputy Gordie parked and importantly led his prisoners inside to the office he was in now, that he was in charge.

"I'll need to question you separately so you'll have to wait in here." And he led them through a door and into rooms separated with bars. With his hand on his gun handle still, he ordered Roma, "Have a seat." She stared at him and silently stepped into the cell, and he slammed the barred door.

"You can't lock us up Deputy?" Daisy yelled looking around for Reed. "You just said you needed us to come in for questioning!"

"Yeah, yeah, but I can't take the chance you might run. They've both got that kind of reputation," he muttered under his breath to his buddies as they stood in the hallway. They too held their hands ready at their hip.

Now Daisy was really pissed. "What?" she whispered. "You just insulted us. You can't do that!"

"Sorry, sorry, now just go in there and be quiet, I've got paperwork to do." Deputy Gordie's voice shook, and his face was hot and sweating.

"You can't lock us up, we're not under arrest!" Daisy protested and stood fast outside the cell door, refusing to go into the room.

The Deputy sucked in his breath and straightened his skinny shoulders. "Miss Daisy I'm ordering you to cooperate or I will have to charge you with insubordination!" He stumbled over the long word.

At that point she decided she better do as the little prick ordered or she could end up imprisoned on some trumped up charge. And where in the hell was Reed, he should have been there by now!

-16-

Daisy sat down on the bench seat in the jail in Birch Lake and sucked in her breath. This was the first time she had been in a place like this for a long time. There was that other time, but she didn't have time to dwell on that now.

For God's sake, here she was fifty- something and a business woman at that, sitting in a cell. Locked up by an ego driven young wanna be. Well, the kid was a deputy carrying a gun, hired by the town's sheriff. But his former duties were only minor situations like looking for lost pets or straightening out traffic jams through town. Now all of a sudden he was thrown into a murder case and Sheriff Montes was off at his cabin for a day of peace and quiet. He had left orders for Deputy Gordie to only call him if a storm threatened to blow the town down. His words! Deputy Gordie had puffed out his chest and saluted his boss. Now finally he could run his town on his own. And he could become famous, world renowned Deputy rules the day! He puffed out his chest again this early morning as he picked out the letters with one hand as he started his paper work sitting at the big desk.

A good thirty minutes went by and the only sounds in the downtown sheriff's office were the clicking of the keys on the computer and the sound of a radio program. A local announcer was listing the price of wheat and soy beans for that day. Daisy listened expecting to hear that Reed Conners had come into the office, demanding to know what the hell was going on!

She should be home dealing with that godforsaken snake. And while she sat there she dialed information on her cell phone for the number of that same nature center that had taken that first snake. The call was answered by a sleepy sounding man. When he heard that another red racer had been found, he perked up and agreed to come immediately and locate the reptile. Now he would have a pair for his nature center he said happily, no doubt dollar signs shown in his eyes.

Daisy smoothed the terry-cloth material in her white pants, and then buttoned the jacket further to cover up the low neck-line on her shirt. She had caught one of the young deputies leering at her cleavage earlier. Her hand then went to her mouth and she bit a nail.

Oh no, she couldn't let that old habit creep back. She had worked so hard to take control years ago. And it sure wouldn't look good for a manicurist to be a "nail biter".

Lord, she thought again, she should be at home getting ready to go up-town and open her shop. She was booked full all morning with manicures and pedicures. Being the only shop for miles around, the summer tourists especially clamored for attention to their fingers and toes. Her prices were high but why not? She had rent to pay and supplies to buy.

She was lucky to share space with Joni, a Birch Lake resident of long standing in the area, well-known around the country as a knowledgeable color specialist and hair stylist. Years ago they had agreed to share several rooms when Joni had remodeled a vacant building and began looking for someone to share the space. Now they worked together and turned out fabulously coiffed and mani-pedied customers. They even had male customers that wanted the same pampered care they were paying for, for their mates. Now, they had been thinking of offering massages and using one of their big closets for the space.

Daisy brushed at her silver hair with her hand and fumbled in her purse for a lipstick, but she shivered as she thought again of her and Roma living with that god-awful snake in her house. Days had gone by and they didn't know! Just where had it been living? And oh my God, they had both gone bare foot many times these last few days.

That bastard that Roma had gotten away from had almost gotten her after all. I wonder how he'll feel when he hears he got Athena killed instead!

As Daisy was fuming over this, she heard a ruckus out front.

"God damn, you've got these women locked up?" She heard Reed Conners exclaim, "You can't do that, they can sue the department!"

Deputy Gordie stood up from Sheriff Montes's large desk. "I'm in charge Reed, and I didn't want them to get away." He held up papers. "Just till I had time to get all this here paper stuff finished."

"Get them!" Reed ordered, and with a look of irritation the Deputy got up and left the room. Then Reed turned to the deputy's friends, who had taken seats. "Guys," he said patiently, "why don't you two take a ride and give us some space." They punched each other and laughed. Then they saw the pissed off look on Reed's face and stood up, but took their time going out the door.

After a few minutes Daisy and Roma burst into the room. He held up his hand to stop the flow of protests he saw on their faces. "I been on the phone with the doc," he said now, "And I've arranged for you to give your statements later today. Come on, let's get out of here."

Roma cussed, and Daisy just shook her head. "And this is my town!" she mumbled.

"I understand there is still one of those snakes loose in your house Daisy?" Reed commented as they got into his Corvette.

"For God's sake yes! I've got someone from the nature center from Minneapolis coming in to collect this marvelous creature as he called it. He should be here shortly. Could you just wait with us?"

"Sure, now do you want me to come with you two when you give your statements later?" Reed asked.

"Jesus yes," Roma said from the back seat. "Or we might be serving time!"

"I don't trust that little shit," Daisy said. "Do you know where the sheriff is?"

"He's at his cabin. I talked to him last night and I'll give him another call today to bring him up. " Reed shifted into second and they left downtown Birch for Daisy's house.

"He should fire his help," Roma insisted. "Now that I intend to live in this town, I might apply for that little pisser's job. I always loved carrying a gun!"

Daisy just shook her head again. "I need to sleep, but it's going to be a long time before I can do that peaceably. How do I know there are not more of these things in my house?"

Reed nodded. "I can understand, Daisy. Snakes give me the "willies.""

"Well, I'm not going back into my house yet. In fact, Roma let's go to the motel after we get done with this guy. It's not the Taj Mahal, but it'll do."

"I'm glad you suggested it," Roma said.

"I've got an idea for you Daisy," Reed said, "I can call an exterminator company and have them go over your house with a fine tooth comb, just to make sure it doesn't have more of those critters in there!" Reed said now as they pulled up on her driveway. A van followed them. "Looks like the guy is here now to pick up your visitor," he added.

Daisy climbed out of his car and hurried over. "I'm Daisy O'Dell, I called you," she said as they walked up to the porch. "I'll let you in and you can go out to the lanai. That's where it is."

"Okay, Miss O'Dell. Do you know where it is out there?" The man held a carrier of some kind in one hand.

"For God's sake no, I just slammed the door after it slithered in there. I'll just wait out here now." Daisy said and shivered. She went back and stood by Reed and Roma next to his car. A good thirty minutes went by and finally the guy came out. His shirt hung outside of his trousers and he had a frazzled look on his face.

"Did you get it?" Daisy asked anxiously.

"Yes ma'am, I did, but I had some trouble getting that second one!"

Roma opened her mouth to exclaim something but slid to the ground in a dead faint instead.

-17-

Daisy and Reed stared at Roma as she lay out cold on the driveway. The man from the nature center had just come out of Daisy's house and proclaimed he'd found two red racers in her house, instead of just one as they'd thought.

They bent down near her. "Roma, wake up," Daisy said. She gently slapped her wrist and ran a hand over her face. "Come on girlfriend, open your eyes!"

They all watched as Roma stirred.

"What the hell--," she murmured. She sat up and looked around bewildered.

"Roma, you're okay, you fainted." Daisy said to her.

"Why?" she asked and looked around for an answer.

Daisy cleared her throat. "The nature center guy had just told us he found two of those snakes in the house."

"Oh hell," Roma murmured again. Daisy helped her stand up a few minutes later.

"Folks," the nature center man went on, "I'm pretty sure that's all now. But do you want me to come back in a few days again?"

"That's all for now." By now Daisy was fed up with the whole situation. She swallowed hard and took her time, then said, "Reed, would you please contact the exterminator company and have them come over today, whatever the cost."

"I can do that," he answered.

"And thank you for coming so fast," she said to the nature center man. "If I see any more of those reptiles, I'll certainly call you."

"For your sake I hope I don't hear from you, but stop in my place in Minneapolis and see my pets when you come down that way." He nodded then and proceeded to his van and stowed the carrier in the back. With a wave he drove off.

The three stood there in Daisy's driveway and looked at the house. "Well," she said, "I wonder how good that exterminator company is."

"I know the guy over there. Daisy, I'll call you and let you know when they can get here." Reed said and turned to go to his car, and then with a wave, he left.

"Roma, why don't you follow me to the motel in your car?" Daisy asked. "It's the only one here right on main street."

"Sure, and I think I will go to bed when we get there. I feel like I've been through rough waters." Roma brushed off her jeans and walked to her rental car.

"I'm so sorry for all this," Daisy called over, then looked at the time. "We'll rest up there, and then I have to shower and get to work by 8:30."

Nopers Motel had been in Birch Lake on the same spot for quite a few decades. Lee and Amy Noper had taken over from his folks when they had handed down the business to them a few years ago. The rooms had been renovated and had new furniture and accessories and the outside had new paint.

Daisy registered when they got there, getting rooms that adjoined. "This way you can have some privacy Roma."

Coming into their new home, they both saw the sign that read, "No smoking."

"Oh damn," Roma said. "Now what?"

Daisy had expected this and said, "There's a cute little courtyard out in back with tables."

"You know, in my country we don't have this silly rule." Roma said, her voice sounding bitchy.

Daisy had to hold her tongue. After all, it was Roma's coming that had started all this, when her boyfriend had tried to kill her by putting the snakes in her suitcases. She looked around now at the motel room. It was nice but it wasn't home. Now even if no more invaders were found in her house, would she ever feel safe? She went in the bathroom and closed the door, then turned on the water. Minutes later she lay back in the tub and closed her eyes.

Damn, damn, damn, she mumbled to the walls. Who the hell was this Muller guy? A killer for hire, Roma had said. And what was the connection between killer Athena and Tom Gulbranson, who owned the funeral home? The more she thought about it the more she realized they would have to have protection.

Getting out of the tub she wrinkled her nose that she had to put on her used clothes, but she had spare things at her shop downtown so she could change when she got there. Thank God, she had her make-up in her purse and took her time now applying the magic formulas she paid big money for. When she finished and came out, she peeked in Roma's room and she was snoring peacefully.

Her shop was just in the next block downtown, but Daisy drove her Porsche over in back and parked. Coming into the beauty shop the familiar aroma of ammonia hit her nose as Joni was busy "perming" one of her ladies.

"Good morning," Daisy said on the way to her quarters. Unlocking her door, here the aroma of acetone floated out to mix with the permanent solution. Several women sat in chairs waiting.

"Good Lord Daisy, what is happening over at your house? Your neighbor, Sadie said someone broke in and you shot her. A woman, who in the world?" Joni asked. Now all eyes were on Daisy, curiously.

She swallowed hard and turned to them. "It's a long story, but right now I've got to get busy." And she called out for Nancy, a summer resident, to come in for her mani-pedi.

The day sped by and Daisy said as little as possible but she did call Reed and asked to meet earlier before going downtown to make their statements. At closing time, she counted her money and locked up. Joni was just combing out her last lady as she hurried out. Daisy waved to her.

"Got time for a margarita?" Joni asked.

"I wish. I've got to check on my friend. I haven't heard from her all day!" Now she hurried down the street to the motel. Inside, she found Roma's bed neatly made and a note on the desk.

"Daisy," she had written, "I'm going to that town you said had a store for women. I don't know what time I'll be back, but soon enough to meet that sheriff for my statement. By the way, I'll buy a new cell phone."

Daisy read the note and felt a sense of relief. Then feeling guilty, she shook her head. Now she had an appointment to see Reed Conners at the local restaurant.

Coming into the Woodsmen, she was greeted by Flo. She knew Flo from the beauty shop where she had her red hair permed and colored on a regular basis. It was said she kept the restaurant running with her strict rules and now her crepe soled shoes swished on the tiled floor as she led Daisy over to a table.

"Here, my dear, you sit now and I'll bring you some coffee." And in a minute Flo was back with a cup and a pot of it. As she filled the coffee she asked, "Is it true you had to shoot a burglar?" Her white nylon uniform crackled as she bent over. And barely taking a breath she went on, "And do you really think those exterminator people can rid you place of that colony of snakes?"

It always amazed Daisy how talk could spread so fast, and just how it always picked up speed as it went along. Now she smiled thanks and Flo stepped back and allowed her to take a few sips her coffee, expecting answers.

"Well Flo, it wasn't me who shot that person that broke into my house."

"No? I heard it wrong then." Flo shook her head. "Who was it?"

Just then Reed Conners strolled in. "My favorite girl," he said putting an arm around Flo and kissing her cheek.

Flo got flustered. "Ohh--," she murmured. "You are such a talker. I'll get you a coffee." And she swished away importantly.

Seeing it might not be a private conversation, Daisy remarked, "Let's take our coffee outside and have a cigarette."

"Might be a good idea," Reed agreed.

A few minutes later, they sat outside under an umbrella in a little fenced off area beside the Woodsmen café.

"Reed, thanks for coming. We have that appointment to meet down at the sheriff's office at 8:00, but I need you to help us on this other business. As we told you last evening, this is about Roma and this man she had an affair with in Oslo. She thought she was getting away from him by coming here, but apparently he knew her plans and put those poisonous snakes in her luggage and then if those didn't kill her, he sent this Athena person to shoot her. He's a killer for hire, you remember!"

Reed lit a cigarette as they sat and then put a booted ankle over a knee. As he listened to Daisy, he swiped his gray streaked brown hair off his forehead. This cool early evening he wore a light blue and white checked shirt with the usual pressed jeans.

"I hope to hell Roma gets back in time," Daisy said then glancing at her watch. "She had to toss all her clothes from her suitcases so she went to Great Falls today to shop." The out-side café was open to the main street and she anxiously watched for Roma's Lexus rental.

"I think Sheriff Montes will be back to take charge by then. He was mad as hell at his deputy for playing hard-ball." Reed blew a cloud of smoke in the air.

"Oh Lord, when his friends came and joined him, I knew we were headed for trouble!" Daisy shook her blonde head. She had repaired her make-up before leaving her shop and changed into a bright pink sundress. It had a low-cut neckline and her wedgies matched perfectly.

"Tell me what you need to charge, Reed and I'm sure Roma will split the cost. I know that this trouble isn't over. When this Gunther Muller learns that Roma is still alive, he's not going to take the chance that she might turn him in to the FBI. He's going to try something else!"

"Maybe so," Reed agreed.

"But Reed, listen, I've had a creepy feeling the last few hours. I feel like someone is watching me!"

-18-

The man sat at an outdoor café in Oslo having his usual cup of dark roast coffee. When the waiter brought his toasted nut bread and cheese, he nodded his head in thanks and set about eating. He didn't engage in any conversation when he was out in public as he trusted no one. The local constabulary had a pretty good force now with that new fresh face outsider they had hired who was from the US. He had read the man had a background as a SEAL.

He dunked his toast in his coffee and sucked out the aromatic liquid and then chewed. His jaws moving rhythmically as his thoughts moved over his day. He felt his cell vibrate in his pocket and taking it out he saw it was from the US.

"Yah," Gunther Muller said in his curt voice.

And not mentioning any names, Tomas Olafson, an acquaintance from the funeral home in the US quickly said, "She got away, but the messenger caught the ball," and then hung up.

Gunther put his cup down with a bang on the metal topped table. Jesus H Christ, he mumbled. How could that be? Roma Hurst should have been dead! Those reptiles should have gotten her, and then if not, Athena was an expert marksman. She should have figured out how to expediently get the job done and abruptly leave the country. No wonder he hadn't heard from the woman, she had gotten herself killed!

Gunther Muller was forty five years old, self taught, cunning and brilliant. Born and raised in Munich by strict parents, he had left the country at sixteen and found his way to Oslo. The landscape was quite different from Germany's stark streets and he never went back. At the time he'd left, he'd stolen all the cash his folks had saved in a tin can he'd found hidden under a board in the floor. He had enough cash then to pay for a room and food for a few weeks, and then he figured he'd get a job working on one of those fishing boats until he got acquainted with the city.

Even at sixteen, Gunther looked older and he started frequenting a neighborhood bar in the warehouse district where he had found a room. Here he kept to himself mostly because he was afraid that the police might be looking for him. However, unbeknown to him, he need not have worried because after seeing he had stolen all their savings, his parents had disowned him.

Soon after moving to Norway, Gunther had met a local woman who took him home with her and where he lost his virginity and quickly learned how to lie, steal and carry a gun. She was much older but he learned to love her, and then realized, it was more a motherly feeling and one day he just left. He had stolen and hidden money again over time and now he went to the affluent part of Oslo and rented a newly built loft. He found the best men's store in town and outfitted himself with class, then enjoyed a day at a spa and got a whole new look, all the while planning his next venture. In learning his craft, Gunther had found the only way to stay out of prison was to work alone. So over time he became a loner. Years went by and he became rich and richer as he silently went about taking from the moneyed. He bought a spacious home that overlooked a fiord, and drove a bullet proof Mercedes. One day, just months ago, as he was having lunch in a café he had seen this beautiful woman sitting by herself. Listening in to her conversation with a waiter, he heard she was trying to tell him in perfect English she wanted only bottled water in her glass, and apparently the local was having trouble understanding her. Her flaming red hair and piercing blue eyes was not lost on Gunther because he only loved fine looking women. So, what the hell he thought, he had time today and went over to her table to help.

"Hello," he said in his perfect English. "Don't you like our water?"

She looked him up and down. "And who the hell are you?"

"Your next lover." He said and laughed.

"Yeah?" She said. "Sure of yourself, aren't you?"

"Always. May I join you?" He asked but already had a chair pulled out.

He liked her looks. He had to have her!

The woman had looked him over with a practiced eye also. She was a single, worldly, well traveled, very rich woman who was very careful. But, what the hell, she had time today too. As he stood at her table, he reached out his hand. "My name is Gunther."

"Hello," Roma said. "You can sit, but you'll have to buy me lunch." She joked, and then laughed. She saw he was very good looking, dressed in a black suit with a gleaming white shirt open at the neck. In a quick glance down at his feet, she saw his shoes were expensive black loafers with tassels.

"I'll even buy you dessert," He shot back and sat down.

"I never turn that down, even though I have to watch my figure."

His eyes went to her low cut neckline. "You're doing just fine!" He ran a hand over his clipped mustache and though he was of German descent and she a resident in her own land, they both spoke perfect English.

Roma liked his gray streaked hair and then caught a glance of his gleaming white teeth as he talked.

"May I ask your name or should I just call you beautiful lady?"

Roma laughed. "You could, but my name is Roma." And after a sandwich and some easy conversation Roma said, "I'm sorry but I have to leave. I have an appointment this afternoon."

"Could we meet back here for lunch tomorrow?" Gunther asked. Jesus, in his profession it was not smart to get close to someone, but just this once, he'd be careful.

That evening as he sat in his book-lined library having a brandy, he put the name Roma Hurst in his computer and was astonished at all the articles it spewed out. How one of their own, Roma Hurst, had come back home to Norway with her millions. And he found she was even richer than him according to the papers. That her ex-husband was a famous US inventor and had made millions on inventions, and, that he had patented another that was talked to be another world renowned addition to the digital world. She had lived in the US and now traveled back and forth. He even saw a picture of a friend named Daisy O'Dell in a group shot at some charity dinner. He stared into space. Was she worth it? Maybe. And he always loved a woman who had money.

Then he studied his next project and it would mean going to China. This one was big! And when he finished this assignment, he was sure he could match her million to million.

That next day Gunther Muller met Roma Hurst at the same café for their second meeting. He had eyed her appreciatively as he approached her table. She wore her flaming red hair fluffed around her shoulders and her neckline was even lower. He had to tear his eyes away from her bosom as he approached her table.

"Good afternoon Roma, you are looking well?" Gunther pulled out a chair.

She had dressed with care today. It had been years now since she'd had anyone to play with and this well dressed, well-spoken man looked promising.

"I am well and thank you for asking." Roma replied and smiled. Soon, before she spent a lot of time with this man, she'd have her journalist friend down at the newspaper check on him and really see who this man was.

"If I ply you with champagne, will you come home with me?" He kidded and winked. God, he had to have her.

"Well, you work fast!" Roma replied. Although she rather liked his abruptness, she wasn't going to be that easy.

Just then a waiter came to their table and Gunther ordered a bottle of their best champagne. Minutes later as they clinked glasses in a toast, he said, "To you, my beautiful lady."

Roma smiled. What the hell, she reminded herself, she had all day. She was back home in Norway and settled in at her apartment. Maybe she'd let this good-looking smooth talking German while away her afternoon.

Several hours went by, and another bottle of wine, and by nightfall she was in his bed where he proved to be an excellent lover.

For the first time, Gunther had found a woman who satisfied him. She was rich and beautiful, demanding at times, but he didn't mind. Over the months they were together, they partied at his palatial home, and not out in public as he said they had everything they needed right there. He had not divulged anything about his life to her, and Roma hadn't asked. She didn't demand to know where he went when he'd disappear for weeks at a time. He had it made; exciting sex, his and her money to throw around, and soon he'd read her ex-old man would be getting millions again when his patent went viral. And Gunther had plans for it!

Months flew by and Roma was having fun. Gunther was exciting and easy going. And rich and independent. At times when he would disappear he would just explain he had a property to check on and she was fine with it. She wasn't about to be tied to anyone and didn't concern herself with his business.

And one day her friend a journalist from the Oslo newspaper returned a call. "Roma, sorry, I've been out of here for months and am just now going over my mail," she said. "You asked if I would look up that man you've been seeing."

Roma smiled as she sat in her bedroom at a dressing table putting on her make-up.

"That's okay, I'd forgotten all about it," she said now easily.

"Roma," her friend whispered, "listen you're in danger. You've got to get away from Gunther Mueller right now. That man is a hired killer!"

-19-

Reed had known Daisy and her family since childhood as their parents had been friends long ago. Decades had gone by as the youngsters had grown up and pursued their careers and then met later as grownups themselves back in their home town.

As they sat now in Birch Lake at the same café they had eaten at hundreds of times over the years, Daisy told him everything since the day Roma was supposed to come to town. How she wasn't at the airport when she had said she would be and then she had shown up two weeks later.

"I was so upset Reed. She appeared to have dropped off the edge of this earth. No phone calls, nothing. I talked to Sheriff Monte about it."

"What did he have to say?" Reed asked.

Daisy shook her head. "He did contact the police in Oslo and there wasn't a missing report out on her there. So there wasn't anything he could do."

"Nothing?"

"Then out of the blue, a few weeks later, she turned up one day," Daisy went on, "Reed, she had been followed by someone onto the plane in Oslo. But she'd gotten away and went into hiding after escaping them from the plane, and finally arrived here dressed like an old woman. She thought she had lost her intended abductors by then."

"So tell me about this Tom Gulbranson, Daisy. I haven't met the man yet."

"Well, Athena Dahl, this woman who died was staying at his house. He's been here in town for a year, I think. I was introduced to them and then she invited Roma and me over for dinner."

"Where was this Tom then?" Reed asked as he blew smoke into the evening breeze.

Daisy sat up straighter in the outside plastic chair. "She said he was out on business, but we both had suspicions even then."

"Why?" He asked.

"Well, for one thing she had previously mentioned to us that she was having a group of people over for an evening. And when no one else turned up, we felt a strange vibe in the air."

"Tell me what you know about this woman, Athena." Reed brushed at the hair that had fallen down over his forehead.

"I don't know anything about her Reed. Or Tom Gulbranson either. He's been accepted by the residents, from what I've heard."

They both were silent and sipped their coffee for a few minutes. The small courtyard outside the café was a designated smoker's area and was busy this evening.

Music was piped outside and Elvis was singing a medley of his oldies and they were both momentarily caught up in the songs.

Daisy said then checking her watch, "I left Roma a note in our room telling her to meet us here when she got back. I hope she didn't forget that we're to meet Jesse tonight to give him our statements." She looked out through the picket fence to the street for the silver Lexus Roma was driving.

"Where did she go?" Reed asked.

"She went to Great Falls this morning to shop. I guess you don't know that she tossed all her clothes, two big suitcases, into the garbage. Everything she brought."

Reed looked at her, not understanding her statement. "What do you mean?"

"Reed, those snakes had lived in her things for days. One in each case."

"Goddamn," Reed exclaimed. "She's lucky she didn't get killed too!"

Daisy shivered, and bumps suddenly appeared on her bare arms. "The only things she had left was the make-up that she carried in her purse."

Reed looked at his watch too. "It's getting close I think we should get over to the sheriff's office. We can ask Flo to watch for her when she gets here."

Sheriff Jesse Montes was at his desk with his shirt sleeves rolled to his elbows. He looked up as they came into his office.

"Hey you two, good to see you again," He looked at Daisy and said, "I hear you've had some trouble again."

"Jesse, I guess you've caught up with what happened." Daisy rolled her eyes as she talked. She and Jesse had known each other for years and were good friends, so she didn't hold back

"I've read the report my deputy filed last night. Sorry, he acted like a know it all and brought you and Roma down here."

"Jess, he was insufferable. Do you know he let his buddies get involved?" Daisy declared still in a huff about being treated like a common criminal.

"Again, I apologize. I figured he could keep things in order but apparently I was wrong. He will be stabilized. Now then, let me take your statement. By the way, where is your friend?" Sheriff Montes asked.

"Roma should be here any minute. She went to Great Falls this morning to do some shopping." Daisy sat up straighter in her chair when she saw the sheriff open a drawer in his desk and take out a tape recorder.

"I will be recording this Daisy, so that I can get this over to the state department. So let's begin, please state your name, address and social security number for the record."

And the interview began. Daisy told of Roma's delay in getting there, and what happened the evening before. It went on for a good hour and when she was through, she looked at the clock worriedly.

"This is not like Roma to not be here," Daisy said. "She is not forgetful."

"Well, let's give her a few more minutes," Jesse was still busy jotting down things in a file.

Reed had been quiet as he listened to Daisy make her statement about the whole sordid episode. "Try calling her, Daisy," he said now.

"I can't," Daisy whispered. Her face paled as she went on. "She tossed her cell away before leaving Oslo, so he couldn't trace her. And purchasing one was one of the first things she was going to do when she got to the falls this morning."

"And you haven't heard anything?" Jesse glanced up from writing.

"No, and I've had my cell on me all day too." Daisy looked at the two men. She had been irritated thinking it was just carelessness on Roma's part, and was going to tell her so, when she got back. But now an alarm was going off.

"Do you know where she was going to do her shopping at Daisy?" Reed asked.

Daisy straightened her shirt as she thought. "Just that she was going to the shops there in Great Falls." As Daisy talked she took her cell phone out of her purse and checked again for any calls. But again there had been none.

"Well, I can get her statement later. For now, I need to get in your house and check out the death scene, Daisy. I understand you feel you need to be with me."

"Jesse, I'm sorry, I wasn't about to relinquish my keys to those guys last night. I didn't want them snooping through my things!"

"Okay, I understand. Do you want to come with me now?"

"No." Daisy replied. "Here's the key and my cell number. But Jesse would you call me when it's safe for me to go home? I need to let the pest control people know it's okay for them to go in and decontaminate."

"Sure, I can let you know tonight if things look good." The sheriff said.

"Thanks, Jesse," Reed nodded. "We'll get out of here and let you do your work, but we'll call you directly when Roma get back."

Daisy and Reed left the sheriff department and walked back to the Café. Flo told them she hadn't seen Roma.

"Where in the world is she?" Daisy exclaimed as they stood outside the Woodsmen Café. "My God Reed, she knew we had this appointment to give our statements tonight at 8:00. I just can't believe this!"

"Daisy, I'm going to get in touch with the department over in Great Falls, and ask them to look for her silver Lexus. But, if she gets back tonight, let me know the minute she gets in, even if it's late, and leave me a message."

Daisy went back to the motel, and after the busy day, she was beat. So she creamed her face and went to bed, figuring she'd hear Roma when she came in. But when she awoke the next morning and Roma still wasn't there, a chill shot down her back. She grabbed her cell and called Reed Conners.

"Reed," she said trying to keep the shakes out of her voice. "Roma did not come back last night!" She ran a hand over her sleep mussed hair.

"She didn't, does she know anyone there in Great Falls?"

"Not anyone that I know of, but she might for all I know. She used to live here too, years ago." Daisy got out of bed. She stepped into the adjoining room just to make sure things were untouched. And same as earlier, Roma's make-up along with pieces of clothing were the same.

"You said she rented that silver Lexus she drives at the airport in Minneapolis, didn't you?"

"Yes, but I don't see any papers here so she must be carrying them with her, Reed."

"Okay, I'll start there, Daisy. Now I would advise you to go about your day, but I want you to be on the alert for any strange cars or strangers around town."

"Reed, do you think something has happened to her?" Daisy's breath caught.

"There's a chance," Reed answered.

"Oh lord, I knew it! With all that's gone on, that attempted kidnapping in Oslo at the airport, killer snakes in her suitcases, then the break-in at my house and the death of that assassin!" Daisy's voice trembled again.

"I'll call Jesse and let him know," Reed said, and then asked, "Did you hear from him last night after he checked out your house?"

"Yes, I did and I can go home. But I've got to meet the pest control people there at 7:00 this morning." Daisy grabbed her crumpled pack of Marlboro's, slipped on a robe and went outside to the little fenced in area. Her hand shook as she put the cigarette to her lips feeling guilty as usual about the habit, but damn, this was not the time to quit!

"Okay, I'm going to track down the information on the Lexus from the rental company and then talk to the sheriff over in Great Falls. I know the guy there."

Daisy nervously took a deep drag on the Marlboro, and then had to steady herself as dizziness seized her. She sat down hard on the metal chair out in the patio at the motel.

"Reed, I have a feeling I'm going to meet this Gunther Mueller. You know, he isn't just going to get rid of Roma. He would assume that she would have confided in me that he was a hired killer!"

"Daisy, do you have a gun and do you know how to shoot one?" Reed asked.

She answered faintly. "I do, I belonged to the gun club here for years."

"Do you have a license to carry?"

"I do." Her voice trembled as she answered. "But I haven't used my gun for awhile. It's a Smith and Wesson 38."

"Daisy, listen to me. The first thing, I want you to do when you get back to your house is get your gun, load it and keep it on you in a convenient pocket.'

"Oh God, it's come to that!" Daisy wailed.

"It has. Now I've got to get going, but I have my cell with me at all times. Call me if anything comes up!"

After he left, Daisy showered and dressed. Today she didn't have time to mess with her hair so she put some gel in it and called it good. Then she grabbed her things and checked out of the motel. Arriving at her house, the exterminators had not gotten there as yet and she did not dare go in. Not even to get her gun, so she sat there in her Porsche and watched the street. After a few minutes though, something caught her attention out of the corner of her eye.

The sun was just coming up and a shadow had moved behind a stand of trees across the street. And flew out into the street.

-20-

Reed Conners had been in his office at sunrise when his phone rang. Finding out it was Daisy was no surprise. He had awakened early with her whole state of affairs weighing on his mind. Was it possible his sleepy small town was going to erupt again with another earth shattering situation? They had just settled down after the Mario D'Agustino debacle.

He had heard the tremor in her voice as she said, "Reed, Roma didn't get back last night!"

He cleared his throat, giving himself a minute to think that through, "Okay, she's been gone twenty four hours now, so I'll put out a missing persons alert."

"Oh God, I'm scared," Daisy had whispered into the phone. "I'll be at my house Reed, then at my shop, but I'll have my cell and my gun with me! Just let some sucker try to get close, and he's dead meat!"

"Goddamn, Daisy, be careful carrying that thing," Reed said. "Now remember don't relax for a minute, keep your eyes and ears open!"

The next thing Reed did then was call Bernard, the computer guy in Minneapolis.

"Hey buddy, how are you?" Reed greeted him. As usual rock music blared in the background and numerous news commentators spoke in unison.

"Hey pison, what's up?" Bernard had been crippled by polio in the fifties and had lived in a chair since. He had established a lost and found business, and could locate anyone, anything, and anywhere!

"Buddy, I need you to find a man. I have a name but no picture. A Gunther Mueller and he lives in Oslo, Norway. It's been said he's a gun for hire."

"That'll take a little time, but he's in here somewhere," Bernard mumbled, already clicking keys.

"I don't have a description, but I would guess he's in his forties or fifties, in good shape and of German descent." Reed paused to drink his coffee.

"Okay, I'm on it," Bernard said then. Reed could hear his wheelchair quake under his weight as he apparently moved around his many computers.

"Okay, thanks Bern. I'll be down there in a few weeks."

"Hey, no sweat, you're one of my good customers."

After Reed was through with his phone calls, he showered and had his last cup of coffee. His girlfriend was at the kitchen table having hers when he came in all dressed and smelling good.

"I need to go into town and take care of some business today Lindy, so I might be gone most of the day." Then added, "But I'll call you."

"Hmm--," she murmured as she reached over and pulled out another chair and put her manicured toes up on it. "What will I do?" She asked, mostly to herself, then.

"Well, I don't know Lindy. You know, maybe it's time you looked up your relatives and reacquainted yourself with them." There he'd said it. He had wanted to before but couldn't find the right time.

Lindy looked at him in alarm. "What are you saying?" She dropped her feet to the floor and shoved the extra chair back under the table. Even the sunflower centerpiece fell precariously close to the table's edge.

"Lindy, I'm just saying you should take the time to go back there and see your siblings." Reed opened the cupboards for a cup, and then saw the contents had been changed around again. "I like that you're here with me Lindy, he said, "but I have a job I have to attend to." He carried his tall cup of coffee from the cupboard over to the table and stopped and kissed her on her cheek on the way out the door.

"Reed, please don't worry about me." She smiled at him.

"I'll call you later. Just make yourself comfortable. It looks like a good day."

He spun the Corvette down through his wooded drive up to the highway and instead of going into Birch Lake he went the opposite way to Great Falls. The small town was another tourist stop with a lake, summer homes and lots of shops. Trendy and spendy was the term he used, but being a small town resident himself now, he gave his many friends free rein to make a living any way they could.

The drive was about twenty miles away and took Reed through the scenic countryside which was filled with hills, wetlands and woods. Countless times he had sped through the area and almost collided with deer as they sprang into the roadside.

Now he remembered and slowed down to an easy 65 miles an hour and soon got into town.

The sheriff department was located right in downtown Great Falls in a brand new building that housed a court house next door. Reed parked and walked in to the offices. A good looking brunette sat at a desk and Reed felt the quick once over she gave him.

"Is Rich in?" He asked her.

Richard Roberts had been the keeper of peace in this town for years. They had known each other from the time they had been kids and he was another person who had chosen to stay in his home town instead of running off to a big city.

The brunette lady stood up and peeked around the corner of the room. "He's in but I think he's just on his first cup of coffee, so be careful. He might still be grumpy!"

She laughed, "by the way," she said and smiling, "my name is Rose and I'm new."

"Reed Conners," Reed said and reached for her hand. A delightful whiff of perfume circled in the air around her.

"This is my first week here and I'm replacing Mrs. Roberts at this job." Rose said then. "I moved here from Minneapolis a month ago."

"You have family then?" Reed asked.

"Boy do I. I have four almost grown kids!"

Reed looked her over quickly and grinned. "Well, you don't look any worse for wear."

Just then Richard Roberts came into the room. "Well, son of a gun buddy, I haven't seen you for awhile now. Where have you been?" He reached out his hand.

"The last few months I've been down in Minneapolis working," Reed said, "but now I'm home for a good long time, I hope."

Rich was a young man in his forties, of Scandinavian descent, standing a good six two, blond and blue. He was known as a stickler for the law in his town and the residents knew it, and a sleepy motorist speeding through soon found out.

"What brings you in?" He asked now.

"Rich, I'm looking for a woman who left Birch Lake yesterday morning to shop here and never came back last night."

"Okay, come on in."

They went in to Sheriff Richard's office. "Have a seat," he invited Reed, "and tell me who you're looking for."

Reed took one of the hard chairs by his desk and sat. "Her name is Roma Hurst. She used to live in Minneapolis but Oslo, Norway, is her home country. She had come here to live."

"Got a description?" Rich asked.

"I'd say she's in her fifties, five-five, one thirty, has long red hair and brown eyes."

"You sound like you know her well, pardner!" Rich winked.

Reed shook his head. "No, nothing like that, I just met her yesterday at a party on a boat."

"Okay, sorry. You said she drove here yesterday. What kind of car does she drive?"

"She has a silver Lexus rental. She got it in Minneapolis from National. That's all I could find out from them."

Rich nodded, "Okay, do you want to do a drive through with me around town?" He asked.

"Great, let's go." Reed stood up and they left the department after Rich told Rose where they were going.

It was going on noon now and the town was awake and busy. The boutiques had their doors propped open to let the potpourri entice eager buyers, and the exhaust from the eatery's sent their aromas of bacon and fried chicken out to the crowded sidewalks too.

As the two men walked out to the special parking place and got in a shiny late model car, the town clock in the steeple above the Lutheran church started booming out twelve tremors of time.

"Doesn't that keep you awake?" Reed asked.

"Nah, it's been doing that for fifty years. It keeps us on our toes." As they talked Rich drove through Main Street, back streets and alleys, around the ritzy neighborhoods and the not so ritzy. Through the town's resident's streets they drove as Reed brought Rich up to speed on the whole scenario.

"Are you saying we could be dealing with a hired killer?" Rich said now.

"That's it, my friend. And get this, when I talked to Daisy this morning she said she thought someone was stalking her."

"Jesus," Rich said and took a cigar out of his pocket and lit up. Then as they took a side road that angled away from town, a dirt, two way with brush and brambles that whipped at the sides of the vehicle. Suddenly Rich jammed on the brakes as the rear end of a silver car appeared through branches hanging on the edge of a deep ravine!

"Goddamn," Reed mumbled, "There it is!"

-21-

Daisy waited outside her house for what seemed like hours, but actually it was about thirty minutes before a truck roared up on her driveway. She had purposely parked on the street and now hurried up to meet the two guys as they stepped down from the cab and looked around.

"Thank you for coming," she said now joining them.

The passenger carried a paper and read, "Miss O'Dell, I see here you have snakes in your house? A nest of them?"

Daisy almost laughed at the absurdity of it. "It's a long story," she said instead. "Two poisonous snakes have been found in there that came here in suitcases. One person was bitten and died."

The two men looked at each other, then shook their heads. "Well, we don't usually deal with this type of invasion, but we do have a remedy."

"Well, whatever you've got I need. I am prepared to stay away for a few days if needed." Daisy said.

"We will have to put out a poison that will draw them to it, and then it needs at least forty-eight hours to work. Then we need another forty-eight to air out before you can go in."

Daisy swallowed hard to still her nerves at this. But what the hell could she do anyway! "Okay," she said then, "now I need one of you to come in with me. It's important that I pick up something from my bedroom closet."

"You sure you should go in there now? Couldn't it wait?" The passenger who seemed to run the show asked. As he stood there in what looked like an undershirt, Daisy got a whiff of perspiration from his direction.

"No, it can't!" She said firmly. "That's why I need one of you to come with and watch out for me."

"Ma'am, we don't usually do that. It could be dangerous."

Daisy was so tired of the whole thing. "This is important, it'll just take me a minute and we'll be out."

"Okay, you go with the lady," the passenger/boss urged the driver. "Take a net along."

As Daisy opened the door and ran to her bedroom, she looked around anxiously. And within minutes she had her Smith and Wesson tucked in her pocket. "Okay guys, I'll be over at the motel or at my shop." And she gave them her card with her phone numbers on. "But tell me what you will be doing?"

"We will be setting out invitations that will draw out any of those critters and poison them. We'll need about four days to be sure."

"Okay, I'll need to lock up after you're done, so I'll wait here." And she went back to her Porsche and got in.

She kept a good eye on their operation as they carried in boxes and cans and thirty minutes later, exited.

"Okay, Ms O'Dell, we're done inside. We decided not to tent your house, but we'll need to come back every day to check on the results. But I'll call you then to meet us here."

That done, Daisy went to her shop and opened for the day. It would be hard to concentrate not knowing where Roma was but today she had coupons she had offered in the daily paper for twenty percent off a set of French style nails, and she had to get busy. Flo, the waitress from the Woodsmen Café was the first lady in her chair having her weekly morning off. She had come in dressed in her crisp white uniform which matched her gleaming white nurse's shoes. "I'm already to go to work when you get done with me," she declared now to Daisy.

"I think we'll be just in time, Flo." Daisy said and put the final coat of polish on her new nails. She led her over to the drying table and set a timer.

Her next customer was a walk in. A man, a stranger who had asked for a manicure, and seeing she had time before her next customer, she had told him to relax and she would be just a few minutes, forgetting Reed's warning.

Now coming back to her small waiting alcove, she saw the man was gone. She looked around curiously. Then it dawned on her.

On my God, she whispered. She clutched the gun in her pocket, and rushed over to the beauty shop.

"Joni, did you see where that man went who was waiting?"

Her friend was in the middle of a perm and said she hadn't, through a mouthful of clips.

Daisy just shook her head and hurried back to her shop where Flo sat intent on admiring her new red nails.

Should she call Reed and tell him about this stranger? Now that she thought about it, what did the man look like? And would she recognize him if she saw him again. All she remembered was that he wore a black shirt.

She went in to her back room, which was only a closet space and slumped down in a chair at her desk. She put her head in her hands and took a deep breath and tried to still her pounding heart. And after a few minutes of concentrated breathing she was able to calm down. Flo's timer went off and she jumped up.

"Thank you sweetie," Flo said and laid her money on the counter. "I need to hurry and get ready for lunch; we're having our weekly roast beef dinner today." She held up her hands and admired her beautiful long red nails. "And oh, I'll need a new pair of plastic gloves now when I clean up after the rush," she murmured as she gathered her bag and jacket and swished out the door.

Daisy's next appointment came in then needing repair on her acrylics and the day began to fly by. New customers with money to spend on their fingers and toes flocked in and she didn't have time to worry about this new guy snooping around her place. It was going on three o'clock when her cell vibrated in her pocket and seeing Reed's name on the ID, her voice began to shake as she answered.

"Daisy," he said, "I've got some news. We've located Roma's car, but not her."

"Where?" She asked, almost relieved now.

"This doesn't look good. We found her car out on a county road, abandoned and locked. We almost missed it as it's in some thick brush and hanging on the edge of a ravine."

Daisy's breath hitched in her throat. "Why on earth?" And her words stuck in her throat.

"We're waiting for a deputy to show up with the tools to open the doors and the trunk."

Daisy's stomach did a flip-flop then for real. "You mean she could be in the trunk?" she whispered.

"We hope not. I'll call you back as soon as we know something." And she heard him click off.

Daisy slid the cell back in her pocket, then felt her other pocket to make sure her gun was safely there. She went back to her customer who was in the midst of getting her new nails French styled. The air was heavy with the tangy aroma of acetone and the small CD player in the corner standing amongst the hundred and some nail polish bottles hummed with the mellow guitar sounds of a local celebrity called Jeffrey, who had made it to the big time.

As Daisy buffed and filed, she remembered she hadn't told Reed about the man who had come in and asked for an appointment and then disappeared. She tried now to recall his description and the black shirt came back but his face didn't. Then she recalled his eyes. It was those eyes that had stunned her. Blue black and piercing. Their conversation had been brief and she had had other things on her mind when he had stepped in the small waiting room and rang her bell. Now damn, why hadn't she paid more attention as Reed had advised?

By the end of the day, Reed still hadn't called back and so Daisy called him but now she got his voice mail. Why wasn't he answering his cell? Had they found Roma?

Her imagination caused her to panic. But she counted her money, locked her doors and then instead of going back to the bleak motel she decided to go at the Legion.

She was at loose ends at being unable to go home, not hearing from Reed and knowing if her girlfriend was dead or alive!

This was the local gathering place, being the only bar in town. There was another restaurant/bar called the Blue Waters that catered to the elite locals and tourists, where the menu was gourmet and where Daisy was a regular, but tonight, she just needed to be close with the people of her town.

-22-

Daisy had not heard from Reed for hours, not since he had called to say they had found Roma's car and that it had been abandoned out on a country road, locked and hidden in the brush. She was worried sick and didn't want to go to the motel and be alone. And she was terribly nervous about that man who had stopped in her shop earlier in the day requesting a manicure, then had disappeared. Had he just wanted to get a look at her, a description?

As she walked into the Legion bar in downtown Birch Lake after closing her nail shop, the liquor establishment was knee deep in locals and tourists. As she made her way through the crowd, greetings were almost covered by the soaring notes of Lee Ann

Rimes as she sang the number one country song called "Blue". The late afternoon crowd was still celebrating their long weekend. Ginger was behind the bar whipping out drinks and when she saw Daisy, she made a tall rum and coke and held it up ready for her. Daisy had refreshed her make-up and put a dab of perfume behind her ears and replaced her sneakers for her high-heeled wedgies. Her short pink uniform looked trim and sexy on her and she smiled at the appreciated whistles.

Ed Harrison, one of the locals, stood up and said, "Daisy, here take my stool. I need to stand up and stretch."

"Thanks Ed. Have you been here that long?" She laughed and gratefully sank down on the stool keeping her purse, squarely in her lap.

"A couple of hours. I've got my dad over on the lot babysitting the new cars; he likes to keep a foot in the business."

"How is the car business this summer?" She asked.

"I'll be in the poorhouse soon if things don't pick up," he commented dryly.

Daisy looked at him in surprise. "I thought you were doing big business over there?"

"Nah, truth be told, but I'm having a blast-off sale starting tomorrow that will run for a week. I'm doing a huge mark down." He took a drink from his beer as he stood by her side.

"Good luck with that." Daisy said. "I just had an ad in the paper and got a ton of new customers." As she talked she tried to take her mind off Roma and what Reed could be doing. She had the gun in her purse, but she still had her cell in her pocket which she had switched to vibrate.

"Daisy," Ed said then, "Would you join me tonight for dinner?" He leaned down closer to her as he asked and she could smell his cologne. Nice, she thought.

Ed Harrison was the local playboy in this part of the county. Single and good looking in his dark skin, he had inherited his mother's middle-eastern features and his father's Scandinavian swagger. He had never married, but she had heard he had come close several times years ago. And he had built a gorgeous house down by the water. She had heard too that he bought all his clothes at the best stores in Minneapolis. And she liked to see a well dressed man and today he was wearing a tan cashmere sport-coat over brown trousers and a pristine white shirt. When she sneaked a look at his shoes, she saw he had on shiny brown loafers with tassels.

With his reputation, she knew he wasn't looking for anything serious. Maybe an evening out would be just what she needed as she knew she wouldn't get any sleep tonight, whatever happened.

"Maybe I'll take you up on that invite, Ed, I'm staying at the motel for a few days, so you can pick me up there." She took a taste of her drink.

"Why, when you have that showpiece of a house?" Then he smiled and winked at her. "But that sounds interesting. Does that mean I might get lucky?"

"Dream on," She remarked playfully, "And I'm not easy. Listen, I'll bring you up to date later on about what's been happening around that house and why I'm at the motel."

Daisy and Ed had known each other since they were kids, having grown up in Birch Lake, although Daisy had left and made her home in Minneapolis and in the twenty five years she had been gone, she had married and raised her family.

Since coming back to her home town to live, a few times in the past they had gotten together and partied but had never gone the "last mile" as Daisy liked to call it. And from what she surmised about him, he was a safe date. He knew she didn't put out, he didn't want commitment, so they would just have a nice dinner together and laugh and joke, and then say goodnight.

"Thanks for the invite Ed," Daisy said then, "I'm expecting a phone call and I'll know then if I can." She checked her cell again and still didn't see any missed messages. "Listen," she added, "if I don't hear something soon, I'm going to give them a call."

"Do you want to go to the casino for dinner? They got a new chef I heard, from Minneapolis."

"Well, it's about time! The last time I was there it was pathetic. The prime rib was awful and the rest of the dinner was bad too." She jumped then as the cell phone in her pocket started to vibrate, and peeking at it, she saw it was Reed calling.

"Oh God," she said getting up off her stool. "I need to take this." And she hurried through the bar and outside.

"Reed hello, what's going on? Have you found her?" Daisy asked breathless.

Reed voice was strained and hoarse as he said, "We did, Daisy," and there was a long pause. "She's gone. We couldn't do anything."

"What Reed? What did you say?" Daisy's legs suddenly gave out on her and she dropped to the curb.

Reed cleared his throat and said again, "Daisy, we found her and she had been killed!"

"My God," Daisy whispered. She blinked tears and caught her breath. "He found her then, this Gunther Mueller."

"Daisy, we don't know anything for sure yet. I'm sorry I didn't call earlier, but I've been with the search party."

"Where did you find her, Reed?" Daisy dared to ask.

"There's a shack about a mile from where we found that rental car. We found her there?"

Daisy sucked in her breath and repeated, "Roma is dead?" Tears sprang to her eyes and she rattled on, not really knowing what she was saying. "My God, and I was irritated because of all this trouble. Reed, I can't believe this, what am I going to do?" She looked up and down the street nervously. Main Street was busy with cars, motor homes and SUVs as tourists and locals were speeding through on their way for a fun filled week-end.

"Daisy, listen to me," Reed said then, "I just talked to Sheriff Monte, and he wants you to come directly to his office."

Chills spread down Daisy's back at the reality of things and she remembered the incident at her shop and said hurriedly, "Reed, I've got to tell you this, a man came into my shop today and asked for an appointment, then disappeared. I'm thinking he just wanted to see who I was."

She could hear him clear his throat again. "Daisy, where are you now?" He asked quickly, and she could hear change in his voice.

"I'm at the Legion, outside on the curb so I could hear you." Her voice began to shake as she listened to his order.

"Daisy," he repeated, "Get back in there now right away. Stay in there with the people and watch for any strangers!"

She stood up and took a step and tested her legs. She ran for the door of the Legion just as she heard him say he'd call Sheriff Monte back.

Daisy clicked her cell off and pushed through the crowd to the bar, to her stool where Ed waited. Her face was white, almost as white as her hair. She fell on her stool.

"Jesus, what happened, bad news?" He asked seeing her shake. Then the bartender came by and he said, "Ginger, get some brandy quick, please," and Ginger expertly poured a jigger and set it down in front of Daisy.

"Whatever kind of news you got kiddo, here drink this." And picking up the liquor he held it to her lips.

Daisy sat frozen in disbelief, grief, then guilt and gratefully sipped. As the burning liquor slid down her throat it helped a little to numb her thoughts. But her eyes teared up for real.

The noise level in the bar rose as another tune erupted from the sound system and Reba came on to tell of her new love.

"What is wrong, Daisy?" Ed asked. "Do you need to go somewhere? I can take you."

Daisy held her tears back and shook her head, then sucked in a breath and said brokenly, "That was Reed, and Roma, my friend, is dead!" She managed to say and put her head in her hands.

-23-

Above the noise in the bar Daisy said, "My friend is dead!" She gulped the brandy down and then Ed heard her say "murdered" under her breath as he leaned down to hear her better.

"Daisy, did you say she was murdered?" He asked

"Hunted, like an animal." she whispered. "And he found her, Oh God, now I know I'm next!" She shrunk down on her bar stool, as if trying to hide.

Ed gaped at her as she lifted her head out of her hands. "What are you talking about Daisy?"

"It's about my friend Roma."

"I met her yesterday on my boat when you two came aboard. Are you saying she's dead, murdered?"

Ed leaned in closer and put his hands on the bar as he talked.

Daisy sat up and swiped at her eyes. Panicked, she looked around the packed bar "Ed, I've got to get out of here!" she said above the noise.

"Okay, where are you going?" He asked and straightened up.

"You don't understand, I'm next, Ed. Her killer could be in here right now looking for me!" She slid off the bar stool and turned to go.

"Hold up, girl." He said and took her arm, and she steered them both to the door. "I'm going with you, Daisy."

As soon as they got outside, and her breathing labored, she said, "Ed no, I don't want to get you involved."

"Daisy, what the hell is going on?" He demanded now.

She turned her anguished eyes to him and gasped. "My friend Roma has been involved with a hired killer from Europe. He followed her here. Now you stay here!"

Then she took off on a run and headed down an alley. If she could just make it to her car that was parked behind her shop, she'd be safe. Two blocks away yet. Damn, her wedgies hurt. Then she stopped for a second and kicked them off, leaving them to scatter amongst the garbage cans and refuse left for pick-up later in the day. On the run again, she got her purse open and grabbed her car keys and her gun.

Oh Jesus, she whispered in her anguished labor. She had never run so fast, or so hard. Her heart pounded ready to explode in her chest. Just another block to go, she saw. Several cars came through the alley, and she caught the fleeting surprised look of the occupants as they slowed down to look. Then her Porsche was there and she pressed her key to unlock the door and just then a hand closed over hers.

Her breath was knocked out of her chest and she clung to the door handle on the car for dear life. Then she heard Ed say," Daisy, for Christ's sake, what the hell are you thinking?"

And she turned and looked askew at him, not understanding.

"Come on," he said and pulled her along. "I've got my truck," and he opened the door to a big black SUV. He pushed her in the driver's door then climbed in and they roared off in seconds.

"When you're on the run it's not too smart to use your own car, Daisy!" He exclaimed.

Daisy just sat in the seat shaking her head numbly wondering what in the world would she do now. It was Friday night, and her things were in the motel since she couldn't get in her house for another day. And she had a full book of appointments tomorrow in her shop and now Roma was dead. Murdered!

She dug her cell phone out of her purse. She had to make some calls, and then she couldn't think straight as to whom. Certainly it wasn't up to her to locate Roma's family, was it? Did she even know where her kids were? Then she just put her head in her hands again and let her tears fall. Crying and whispering, Oh God, oh God!

After a few minutes, Ed reached a hand over to her shoulder. "I really don't know what's going on Daisy, but I'm making a quick stop and then taking you over to my house. You'll be safe there."

Daisy raised her head and looked around. They had sped out of town and now Ed drove into a farm yard and into a barn, then pulled her out of the SUV, sat her in a car, and they were back in Birch and headed down to his lake home in minutes.

"See, an easy exchange and the black hornet disappeared," he snapped his fingers and tried to smile at her.

Daisy sat up and wiped her eyes. She had never been to Ed Harrison's house before. It was a one story red brick with white trim. The landscaping was professionally done with shrubs and rock, and a huge cluster of white birch shaded the bright white front door. They sailed into a garage tucked onto the rambling building.

When the motor stopped, Ed took her hand and said, 'Come on Daisy, you'll be safe here." He gently pulled her out of the vehicle and they went up a few steps and into a vestibule, then into a kitchen. He motioned her to a chair at a table.

"Do you want a sandwich or a glass of wine?" He took off his sport coat and rolled up the sleeves of his white shirt.

Daisy sat down, then looked at her bare feet and exclaimed, said. "My God, I don't have my shoes!"

"Well," Ed said looking at her and attempting to make her smile. "I've got some you can borrow and we can put some T. P. in the toes to make them fit!" He opened a door into what looked like a wine cellar with a high top table and chairs in the middle of the room and went in.

"Come on in Daisy. This is my second home," he laughed as she tiptoed across the tiled floor and looked around at his collection of bottles. "I'm a collector as you can see."

"Wow, I didn't know that about you, Ed."

He took a bottle off a shelf. "This is a nice brandy. Let's go sit down in my living room and I want you to tell me everything," and he motioned her to follow.

Still holding her purse close because the gun was there, he led her into his living room.

"Okay, Daisy, sit and finish that story. I have security over every inch of this place, no one can get in." And seeing her shiver he picked up an afghan and put over her shoulders.

By now Daisy had enough time to get over her tears, and she sat on a couch with her bare feet tucked under the cover for warmth.

"Are you sure you want to get involved? You are putting your life in jeopardy."

And Ed being who he was said valiantly, "Just let some asshole try anything, and he'll land on his ass so fast he won't know what hit him!"

Daisy just shook her head. "He's a hired killer Ed. You just don't know."

"How the hell did your friend get mixed up with this guy?" Ed carried two brandy snifters over and poured the amber liquor. He held one out to her and she took a drink and then felt the fire in it warm her insides.

"What many people don't know is that Roma was, a very rich woman."

"He wanted her money? Why, if he is what you said he is, he must be a frigging millionaire!"

"Roma said he's crazy, that he was out to get even with her for leaving him. Thank you Ed but I can't stay here. I need to go somewhere."

"Daisy, be reasonable, where would you go?"

Daisy swallowed again. "Well I don't know," she said slowly. "But, he'll find me here too if I'm next on his list."

"Jesus, woman, give me some credit. Sit right there, and I'm going to make some calls." And he left the room for a few minutes. Coming back and sitting down, he declared. "Sit tight, inside of ten minutes there'll be men with rifles outside watching for anything or anyone trying to get on this property!" She didn't know that he had called Sheriff Monte who put in an urgent call to the National Guard for help in guarding the town and the citizens against a terrorist's attack.

At this point Daisy could not protest any longer. So she leaned back on the couch and let the brandy soothe her frayed nerves. As yet she just couldn't comprehend that her friend lay dead somewhere and that she would never see Roma again.

Somewhat tipsy by now, she wondered what would she do with all those bottles and jars of her make-up that stood in their room over in the motel.

-24-

Reed Conners stood with the search parties as they waited for details from the coroner surrounding Roma's death. They were out in the woods a few miles from the town of Great Falls where she had been found in a run-down old abandoned farmhouse. Her silver Lexus had been located, pushed off the dirt road just a mile from there. The dozen men in the search parties were volunteer firemen from the county who had been trained to act promptly in any catastrophe and they were all gathered now awaiting dismissal after locating the missing victim.

They had painstakingly followed tracks found in the dust on the road that led into the woods, and it hadn't taken more than several hours for Reed and his search party to locate Roma's body after finding the vehicle. After seeing what appeared to be two sets of footprints, he figured she had been forced to walk into the woods more than likely at gun-point. What he didn't know at first was why had the killer brought her here. Then he had seen the cigarette burns all over her body, and knew the bastard apparently wanted to have some fun with her first and make her suffer.

The run down house stood in a weed infested yard bordered with a grove of trees on three sides. It was a two story salt-box covered in faded green tar-paper. The ragged edges had curled and the color had faded to a grey over most of it and all the windows were broken. As the search party came into the farmyard, they had first searched a barn, precariously leaning to the side, and then found tracks through the weeds leading to the house.

As Reed pulled the rusty broken door open, he stepped into what looked like a kitchen and as if someone had just up and left everything behind. An old wood cook stove stood against a wall, dirty white cupboards hung haphazardly against another. Doors stood open on them and dishes and cans lay amongst bird nests. A family of squirrels had chattered at him from under a table that lay upturned and leaning sideways. Leaves and dirt lay over everything. Then he saw tracks leading through the refuse, and up a narrow stairway. First testing the steps for safety, he hurried up taking two at a time. Up there too, dirt and leaves covered ancient furniture scattered everywhere. Chests lay on their sides with broken drawers close by, and the iron bed frames were still there, with mattresses torn and dirty on the floor.

This was where he found Roma. Her clothes were torn and lay scattered amongst the dirt. As he bent down to her, he could see she had been tortured by cigarette burns all over on her body. He swore under his breath. Then he saw the awful wound around her neck and realized she had been garroted by a fine wire that had cut into her throat, which lay close by. He stepped back from the blood-soaked mattress and gagged.

He had met Roma twice and that was a few days ago on Ed Harrison's boat and then last evening when Daisy had brought her along to his place, when they had wanted him to help guard against this crazed killer. She had been a well built redhead, filling out a t-shirt and shorts. She had winked at him when Daisy had first introduced her to him.

"Come on," he said to the three guys who stood silently gaping at the nude body.

And then, white faced and sick looking, they all scampered down the stairway and hurried outside and sucked in the fresh air. He reminded them this was a crime scene, and to stand in one spot and not move around and mess up any of the tracks. He called Sheriff Montes on his cell and they had all stood in shocked silence and waited for the other search parties to join them.

This is where he was when he called Daisy and told her they had found her friend. He hadn't given her any details and she hadn't asked, but he would have to tell her soon.

The men were quiet after seeing the murder site. For some, the newly recruited men, this was their first actual event and they were appalled at the grisly scene. Just then one of the men in the group sank to the ground and started gasping for a breath. Reed hurried over, and put a hand on his shoulder.

"Take it slow and easy buddy," he said calmly. "Take a breath, and it'll go away." And he stood by the man, who was a young married family man named Freddy from Great Falls, and soon Freddy's color returned and he stood.

Jesse Montes and Sheriff Richards from Great Falls had joined the coroner upstairs in that old house after they had taken a statement from Reed. Now he waited for them to come back out and release the search parties, so the guys could go home.

It was now going on sundown, the close of the second day after Roma had been missing. Reed tried calling Daisy on her cell phone, but didn't get an answer. He'd gotten the message from Sheriff Montes that Ed Harrison had taken her to his house, but that didn't mean she was absolutely safe even there in his locked compound.

Goddamn, but he felt terribly remorseful. He hadn't really thought this was as bad as the women said. After all, when would a killer for hire come to this part of the country? It wouldn't happen. But, then when he couldn't get much sleep last night thinking about it, it wasn't too much of a surprise when Daisy had called and said Roma had never come back home to Birch Lake from her shopping trip to Great Falls. His gut must have been trying to tell him something.

Sheriff Montes came out of the house then. "Okay, here's the deal," he said wiping his brow with a hanky. "Sheriff Richards has to stay with the coroner until the BCA; the crime lab from Minneapolis arrives. I need you to gather at my office for new orders. On the way, as you are aware I'm sure, but let me remind you, not to talk about this to anyone. We will release information to the news when we have something concrete to divulge." And the men turned to go, with some furtive glances back at the remembered scene.

"When do you think this took place?" Reed asked Jesse now when they were alone.

"We think it must have been sometime yesterday morning from the looks of the body." Sheriff Montes wiped his brow again. "God almighty, she was almost decapitated," he mumbled.

Reed swallowed hard. What the hell? He turned away from his friend. Was he going to be sick? Goddamn, he had been in the business in some way all his adult life and had seen a lot. Now, like that new recruit, the grisly scene threatened to rip out his insides. Then thankfully, after a few more minutes he was able to gain control and he turned as Jesse declared. "Now we need to concentrate on finding this mad man."

"I need to contact my friend who has been doing research on this asshole." Reed said then and dialed Bernard, his computer guy.

When Bernard came on the line, he said. "Yep buddy, I'm guessing you have a full blown killer on your hands. I recommend calling in all the troops in your part of the country."

"So, what did you find?" Reed asked.

"Not a hell of a lot." Bernard complained. "The psycho hasn't left a trail, but I found out from an acquaintance in Europe that he might have ties to the CIA, as an anti-terrorist agent."

"You're kidding." Reed commented under his breath. "You mean he's legit?"

"Yes and no, but if he is, he goes both ways buddy. Anyway you look at it, he's bad news."

Reed clicked off his cell and said, "Jesse, we've got to get the cavalry out there fast. We've got big trouble!"

"What now?" Sheriff Montes asked curiously after Reed's comment.

"Jesse, my contact says he may be one of those bad-ass secret agents working both sides of the law."

"God almighty, you mean a spook, a retired Fed turned bad?"

"That could be who we're dealing with." Reed swiped a hand through his hair, then bent down and brushed some thistles off his pants legs.

"Okay, we've got to get back to Birch. Come on, I'll run you back to your car Reed." And the two men hurried to the official vehicle.

On the way back, Reed made a call. "Hey Ed, are things quiet there?"

"Yup, I've got things locked down. Three of my buddies are outside with rifles watching the house." Ed's house sat on several acres of land edging up to the water.

"How's Daisy?" Reed asked then.

"She's out like a light here on the couch. I made her drink a little brandy and that finally did her in. What's happening out there now Reed?"

"Get this, we are dealing with a stone killer! Don't tell Daisy this, but the asshole almost decapitated Roma. We found the ligature he used. He tortured her with cigarettes first!"

"Aw-- Jesus." Ed grumbled.

"Jesse and I are on our way back to Birch. We've got the search crews meeting at his office in a few minutes again for further direction."

"Okay, I've got my 45 next to me and she's safe." Ed said and clicked off his cell.

Just then Daisy sat up and threw the covers off and exclaimed, "Ed, take me back to my house. I need to go home!"

"Sorry lady, you're not going anywhere!"

-25-

As soon as Daisy's eyes opened she remembered what was going on. When she heard Ed say she wasn't going anywhere, she stood up throwing the cover to the floor.

"My God, what's going on? Why did you let me sleep?"

"Daisy, relax, you needed the rest. I just talked to Reed and now here's what we're going to do." Ed got out of his recliner. "Reed wants you to sit tight, so I've got a swell guestroom that never gets used for you to camp out in."

Daisy looked at her watch. "But I can get into my house now. There's been enough time for it to get aired out after the exterminators were there."

"That might be true, but he said for you to stay put. He doesn't want you to leave here."

"Why?" Daisy ran her fingers through her hair, straightening the silvery hair-cut.

"Because there's a manhunt going on now for this Mueller," he said as they stood in his TV room, facing each other.

"But I've got my gun," she protested.

"Daisy, listen to me. Sheriff Montes has issued a lock down on the town. No one is allowed to venture out tonight."

"Oh God," Daisy whispered and sank back down on the couch. She clutched her arms around herself. "He's looking for me now, isn't he?"

Ed put a hand on her shoulder. "Listen, you're safe here. I've got men right outside watching every inch of this place."

Daisy looked around the room doubtfully, at the windows and the door that led out to a patio. A shudder went through her as she realized the killer could be right outside, waiting. Just waiting for her!

"Come on, let's go to the kitchen and find something to eat." Ed said then noticing her anxious glance at the many windows. "I want a steak, how about you?" He slipped his loafers on and led the way.

It was going on midnight now as they walked through the house and even though Daisy was overwrought with emotions she noticed his tastefully decorated surroundings.

"I like your place. It looks every bit as good as mine." She tried for some relief in the somber night.

"We probably had the same designer." He motioned her to a stool at the marble topped counter, and then turned on a low light.

"Did Reed tell you anything about Roma, and how she died?" Daisy asked. "Was she shot?" Her face crumbled, and she put a hand over her lips to still their trembling.

Reed had told him the gory details, but he didn't have the heart to elaborate.

He said now, "We can find out in the morning. Daisy, how about you make a salad and I'll tend the steaks." He had turned on the grill on the gas stove, then the vents a few minutes before and now the NY cuts sizzled.

Daisy still had on her pink uniform and she had borrowed a pair of wooly socks. She had her .38 in the pocket and had kept it hidden from him, by slipping it under a cushion in his couch. Now he said, "Daisy, take that goddamn piece of yours and put it on the counter."

She looked at him sheepishly for a moment. "Okay, it was making me more nervous anyway." And she laid the handgun on the countertop and began to tear up the lettuce and slice the vegetables he had taken out of the refrigerator.

Her thoughts were scrambled. If only she could get home to her own house. It felt like weeks since she had been getting ready for Roma's visit. Cleaning and shopping for new sheets and towels and planning meals. All the drama that had taken place since her arrival was astounding. And now she was dead.

"I wonder who will notify the family," she commented worried now, almost to herself. Then said, "Roma has two sons, but I don't know where they live. Should I call someone and at least give out their names?" She looked at him expectantly.

Ed flipped the steaks and then the seasoned goodness surrounded them in the kitchen. Taking two plates out of the cupboard he slipped them in a warming oven. He turned to her, "I'm not sure Daisy, maybe you should just wait until morning and then call Sheriff Jesse's office girl and she'll know what to do."

"Yeah, maybe you're right." She put the finished salad on the table and just then he had the steaks ready and brought the steaming plates to the table.

"Come on, Daisy, you need to eat something."

She sat down but as she looked at the food, her throat closed up. She drank some water and choked. "Oh God, I can't." She whispered hoarsely.

He looked at her for a minute. "If you can't, at least just drink some more water. I can make you a sandwich later."

Daisy sat at the counter and watched him wolf down the steak. It was late and she was a mess of nerves. No way would she sleep tonight either. That little nap she had earlier took care of that.

"Sure you can't even try some salad?" Ed asked?

"Thanks," she said. "Maybe later."

Done now with his steak, he stood up. "Come on, I'll show you one of my guest rooms." And she followed him down a hallway, by many doors opening into various settings. Then he opened one into a lovely decorated bedroom of lavender and lace.

"Wow," Daisy murmured standing back.

Ed smiled. "Years ago this was my mother's room."

Daisy hesitated after seeing the things around that apparently belonged to her. There was a book and reading glasses on the bedside table. A robe lay over a footstool.

"She's been gone for years but I've just left these things here."

Daisy could see right off she couldn't get into that bed. And not wanting to hurt his feelings, she asked. "Do you mind if I use the shower in here to freshen up, then, if you've got a sweat suit I could borrow?"

"Sure, there's towels and soap. And I'll find you something to wear but, you'll swim in it." And he took off down the hallway.

The minute he left the room, she closed the door. Now, at last alone, she couldn't keep her tears at bay any longer. She stood inside this beautiful room that held memories of another dead lady and began to cry. She sobbed brokenly for the loss of her friend, for the unjustness of her loving a cruel and dangerous man, for the sorrow Roma's sons would feel at her death. She even cried for her own impatience at her friend's problems. Her tears ran uncontrolled down her face. She was too overwrought at this point to notice a face try to see in through a crack in the window's shade. Or see it dart away. Suddenly the light in the room went off, along with rest of them throughout the house.

Her tears turned cold. She stiffened. Then instinct sent her to rolling over the bed and falling into the space by the wall and crunching down. She lay quietly and hardly dared to breath. Seconds went by and she tried to listen.

Who had turned off the lights? Where was Ed?

When she had landed on the floor behind the bed, her right hand had gotten twisted under her. Her gun was still in her uniform pocket and now she tried desperately to untangle herself and get a hold of it. Then, finally she had it in hand. As her eyes became adjusted to the near darkness, she dared raise her head an inch over the pile of decorator pillows. She saw nothing. A few minutes slipped by. She didn't dare let her attention drift off. Then, as she stared into the murky shadows the door opened slowly, soundlessly.

Her breath caught in her throat and she steadied the gun with both hands.

A dark figure crept into the room. And in that instant she saw it was the man who had come into her shop that afternoon and then disappeared. The movement and the shape of the stranger spelled killer to Daisy as he came toward the bed. She raised the .38 then and pumped shot after shot at the target.

She saw the figure slump and felt the movement when it landed on the bed. She didn't know she had continued to pull the trigger until it echoed its emptiness in the room or how long she had sat there in the corner, but then the room was suddenly flooded with light and Reed burst in.

"Goddamn, Daisy where in the hell are you?" he yelled. "Are you okay?"

"I'm here," she said faintly and crawled out from her hiding place.

He gave her a quick once over. "You got the fucker! Thank God, you were lucky, Daisy." Then, bending over the bed to get a better look, he commented, "Well, here he is, the notorious Gunther Mueller."

Daisy straightened up, then looked down at herself in horror. Blood covered the front of her pink uniform.

Then Reed turned from the grisly scene and held up what he had taken from Gunther's hand. It was another ligature!

-26-

Daisy stared in horror down at her blood splattered uniform, and then gaped at Reed as he held up a circle of wire. The silvery thread he'd taken out of Gunther's hand without thinking glimmered in the ceiling light.

"What the hell is that?" Daisy asked, but knew what it looked like. "Is that--?" Her face was ashen as she stared at it.

Reed had stuck his gun in his waistband after he had burst in the room. He had seen the man's body explode as bullets from Daisy's gun pelted him. Knew he was dead instantly.

"It's called a ligature, Daisy and he would have used it on you. Goddamn, now I've got my DNA on it!" He laid it down carefully on the bed, and then repeated. "I've got to call Jesse."

Daisy glanced hurriedly at the bloody sight on the bed and nodded her head in that direction. "How did he get inside with all the guns out there?"

Reed wiped his face on his shirtsleeve. "The fucker was cunning. He watched and waited for each guy to be alone and crept up and apparently used some kind of weird dead lock. I found two men out cold. He got in a window and found the fuse box."

"How did you know he was in the house?" Daisy wanted to know.

"I had just gotten here when the lights went out, and then we found the guys. We knew then he had gotten in."

In minutes Sheriff Jesse rushed into the room, his gun raised. He yelled, "Where is he?" He furiously looked around, then saw the bloody body and rushed over, his gun pointed. "God almighty," he roared, "He's dead!"

"Yeah, Daisy got him." Reed exclaimed.

Jesse's cap had fallen off as he rushed into room, and as he lowered the gun and bent over to pick it up, he groaned from the extra exertion. Beads of sweat glowed on his face.

"You're hurt, Daisy?" he said straightening and seeing her blood stained uniform.

Daisy stood stiffly, afraid to touch her dress. "No, I'm okay Jesse. He almost fell on me." Her hair was askew and her face was almost as white as her hair.

A female officer from a neighboring town arrived and after a brief conversation amongst the group, Sheriff Jesse asked her to take Daisy out and find a room for her to change in. "Would you be so kind as to bring in the clothes we carry for emergencies, for her to put on."

And in relief Daisy followed the woman out of the room. They found a bathroom and Daisy hurried in and dropped her blood soaked clothes on the floor.

"I'll be back in a few minutes with those things for you to put on. They're probably not very fashionable but they're clean." The officer said and as she walked away her accessory filled belt jingled.

Daisy did a quick cat wash. And in a few minutes the officer was back and handed in a bundle containing a gray sweat suit.

"I've got to find Ed," Daisy said then hurriedly. "Did you see him?" she asked the officer.

"I don't know who you mean. I'm sorry." They went to the kitchen and there, people were gathered around someone on the floor.

As they came closer Daisy whispered, "Oh no--," when she saw Ed was the one on the floor and paramedics working on him.

She stumbled in her haste, and then limped closer as she saw he was so very still.

She covered a sob with her hand and sank to her knees and looked on in unbelief. This man whom she had known all her life had just given up his life for her. And he had done so with his usual bravado and show.

She watched numbed with sorrow, as the medics administered to him. Then to her astonishment he started moving. The medics sat back for a minute. Then got busy again disconnecting wires and tubes.

"You're back buddy," One medic declared.

Ed groaned and tried to move. Then he mumbled, "What happened?"

"Apparently you were zapped."

"A stun gun? Jesus, I didn't even see anyone." He whispered hoarsely. "Is Daisy—?"

"I'm here." Daisy said and came over closer where he could see her. "Are you okay?"

"Yeah?" Was all he could manage to say. His body hurt all over.

"Ed, I shot Gunther Mueller and he bled all over your Mom's bed!" As the words traveled over her lips, Daisy wondered why she didn't feel any remorse at killing a person. She'd have to think about that.

Ed whispered, "He got in even though I had those guys out there? I'm sorry Daisy," he whispered as he lay on the floor. Then he took the oxygen mask off his face. "I'm okay now guys, thanks." And he sat up, and then slowly stood, amidst caution from the medics. Daisy took his arm and together they walked slowly and carefully into his living room where they sat down on a couch. The same one she had been on just hours ago.

"Well now Daisy Mae," He said after getting his strength back and using the name he used to call her in their school days, attempting to lighten the moment. "Do you want to stay here with me for a few days?"

"Thanks Ed, but I need to go home and check on my house. But I am so sad that my friend won't be there and had to die because of that mad-man. Poor Roma, she was so looking forward to living here in Birch Lake. She said once she was going to buy a boat, a fast one."

Ed put an arm over her shoulder. "I'm sorry Daisy. But I don't want you to be alone now. I could stay with you."

And suddenly she did feel forlorn and alone, which was different for her. Normally she was upbeat, independent and sometimes even a wiseass, and this feeling was new to her. She put her head back and moved closer to him and they sat like that for awhile feeling the comfort and warmth of each other's company.

After some time, Reed and Sheriff Jesse came into the room. Reed took an easy chair and Jesse found a spot on the opposite couch.

"Ed," Jesse said now, "Doc took the body out and we have closed off the room. The BCA will be here in the morning to do whatever the hell they do." He wiped his brow and tiredly blew out a breath. "I sure could use a cold beer," he grumbled, "but I've got hours of paperwork to do yet tonight, or I should say, this morning."

Seeing his friend Jesse unusually tired, Reed added, "I'll come with you and keep you company Jesse. Come on," He said. "And when we get done we'll have a couple."

"Man that sounds like a good idea." Jesse stood up and jammed his cap back on his head. "See you tomorrow then Ed. I'll probably have to come back with those people."

"You can call me on my cell," Ed said.

Daisy sat up after they left and frowned. "I've got to leave too. I can get back in my house now. But I'm trying to remember where I left my car, for God's sake. It seems like days ago."

"We'll take mine and go look." They leaned on each other as they left his house.

And they found her car just where she had left it in the parking lot by the Legion club. The birds had started to sing in the daybreak as Ed followed Daisy to her house.

Daisy drove the Porsche into the garage and walked to his car. "Come on in Ed," she said and unlocked her door and they stepped in to her foyer. She stood still and looked around, then shuddered. "Oh Lord, will I ever feel safe in here again? Ed, I've got to check first to make sure there aren't any more of those critters in here," she added under her breath.

Ed took her by her shoulders. "Daisy, you put the coffeepot on and I'll check the house. I promise I'll look in every nook and cranny."

They walked into the kitchen where all the cupboards stood open and empty. "Thank God I keep my coffee in the refrigerator," she said faintly. Suddenly, she felt as if her movements and her words were coming from somebody else. Her world felt surreal.

Ed had slipped on a pair of faded jeans and a black t-shirt before they left his house. And he reached under his shirt now and pulled out a gun. "See Daisy," he said, "I come prepared."

-27-

Daisy warily looked around her kitchen as she and Ed came back to her house. This was the first time she had been back there after all the commotion. First she had excitedly planned for Roma's visit and awaited her arrival and now she was dead.

How could things have gone so wrong? The sadness of losing her friend finally caught up with her and she sat down on a stool at the counter and began to cry. Hard soul felt sobs and she lay her head down on her arms. Ed came back into the room after checking the house for any more marauding snakes and alarmed, put his arms about her and pulled her up into his arms

They had known each other in school decades ago and had run into each other as adults over the years, but had never spent time together. Now her slim body seemed to fit comfortably right into his as her sobs and tears wracked her frame.

"Daisy, I'll help you through this," he whispered, then reached over to a box of tissues. Soon her tears subsided and she stepped away and blew her nose furiously.

"Oh nuts, I'm sorry Ed." She said in a hoarse voice, "I'll be okay." And in that moment she recognized an arousal in her body. She forced her thoughts to the issue at hand and went on to say, "I know you checked the bedroom Ed, so excuse me for a few minutes while I grab some clothes."

The delicious aroma of fresh coffee permeated the air even as far away as her bedroom suite as she slipped on shorts and a tube top and hurried back to the kitchen to where Ed was. He looked at her anxiously.

"I'm fine now, Ed," she said, "Thanks for being here, but I'm sorry you had to witness my outburst." Reaching down in the cupboard, she took out a thermos.

"Daisy, you don't have to apologize. I'm just glad I was here with you."

Her hands trembled as she tried to pour the coffee in the small opening at the top of the canister. "I'll take this with to work," she explained.

Taking the hot coffee pot in one hand he continued to fill the thermos. "Listen, I have gone over your house with a fine tooth comb Daisy, and I would declare it safe and free of any more of those damnable critters." Ed stood across from her at the granite covered center island.

Daisy had gelled her blonde hair and swept it up and off her face. Devoid of make-up now she looked like a young boy sitting there. She shivered and darted glances to the corners of the room, then at Ed's face as he talked.

"Okay, but I've got to go in and open my shop this morning and I imagine you've got your place to open."

"True," he kidded, "but we could play hooky for a few hours. We could go out in my boat and just cruise?" He winked at her.

Daisy thought about that feeling of unrest in her limbs. Ed Harrison was the town bachelor and rich. She looked at his six foot tall frame with some interest. He was good-looking, with black hair and brown eyes, and he did work out because she'd heard he had a gym in his house fit for an athlete and he was trim.

"What are you thinking Daisy Mae?" He asked jokingly. "Too soon?"

"Well, a little," she said weakly, not ready to go there yet and then went on, "Ed, I'm going to go back to the motel and then open my shop, as I've got a full house of appointments to take care of this morning." She stood up.

"Okay, I'll follow you to see you get there safely." He stood up too and began to put things in the dishwasher. "See, I make a good wife!" He said trying to lighten the moment and winked again at her.

Back in her bedroom, Daisy opened drawers for her underclothes and then hurriedly grabbed hangers of things out of the closet. On her way back to the kitchen she stopped in the bathroom for her makeup bag.

"I'll get ready for work over at the motel," she exclaimed.

Ed looked at her, but didn't question her why she was in such a hurry to leave her house. "Okay," he said. "But would you like to meet me and get a bite to eat later today?"

"Maybe." she murmured as they walked to their cars not at all sure if she would pursue this venture of getting to know him better. Then she climbed in her Porsche and sped away leaving Ed to maneuver his black SUV around her drive.

At the motel she hung her clothes and put her make-up on in the small bathroom. It was the height of the tourist season and the town was buzzing with activity. Her book was full with manicure and pedicure appointments and she had called in the high school girl again today to give her a hand with the phone. She happened to glance down at the list of names for the day and to her surprise saw a man scheduled for an hour. It wasn't unusual for a man to come in, but the name Ron Randall startled her.

Just what did he want this time?

-28-

"It was self-defense so that settles it," Sheriff Jesse Monte said to Reed Conners as they left Ed Harrison's house in Birch Lake and proceeded to the sheriff's office. The coroner, who was also the town's medical examiner and who owned one of the funeral homes had picked up the body, and now the BCA was there taking samples. Jesse had placed his deputy at the door at Ed's house to watch for strangers who might try to get in the house or on the property and to lock up after everyone was through with their business. Ed had left earlier with Daisy to pick up her car.

"And now I have another stranger's body in my town." Jesse went on to comment as they came into his office.

"Any calls?" he asked his young officer in training who had worked the night shift, as he stopped at her desk. She handed him a stack of pink slips which he absently stuffed in his shirt pocket.

"I wonder if we should contact the FBI, Jesse," Reed said then as he brushed at his hair.

"God almighty," Jesse groaned, "I'm thinking the same thing. Remember MacGreger? He was the one who helped solve that D'Agustino case."

"Good man. I remember him well. I'd say give him a call."

Reed followed Jesse into his office and sat down in one of the straight backed chairs in front of his desk. The sun was coming up and the birds were chirping their hearts out in a morning song. It had been a long night filled with horrors ending with Daisy shooting and killing Gunther Mueller.

Jesse turned on his laptop and after locating MacGreger's number punched it into his cell. After a minute he got a canned message saying to leave a number. "Well, you would think they'd have 24 hour service." He mumbled and clicked off, then began the task of filling out all the necessary forms about the night.

"How about I make some coffee?" Reed offered and went to the sink in the cupboard off to the side and filled the electric pot with water and coffee grounds. While that was perking and sending out the delicious aroma, he casually mentioned, "Do you think we should send inquiries to Europe? We do know he's from somewhere over there."

"Yeah, I figure I can do all that with the help from the FBI. And then I need to know where to ship the body. He must have a family somewhere."

After an hour of filling out the necessary forms on his laptop about the shooting, Jesse stood up and stretched. Reed had filled out his report too about what he had walked into, which he knew he would have to go over again and again.

"Come on, I can smell the bacon Stan is cooking up next door, let's go over and have breakfast," Jesse said. "Anyway, I can't do any more until I hear from the big guys."

"I'll be next door at the café so you can send any calls to my cell. I'll be back in an hour." He advised his girl in training.

Over at the café, the two men took a seat at the counter. Some of the locals were already there and immediately started to question Reed and Jesse.

"I hear Daisy shot a foreign spy?" One commented. "Nah," another added, "she is dead, shot by some gun crazy yokel from Europe." The guys at the Woodsmen Café repeatedly chewed over their comments and waited to hear more. Reed looked at

Jesse as Flo placed coffee down on the counter for them and said, "Jesse can fill you in."

Jesse grumbled under his breath. He liked his buddies but he was stressed to the limit. Now that his retirement was coming up he wanted to ease out of his elected position in good standing. "I can't release too much yet," he said, "but I can say the stranger with the gun is dead, and Daisy is fine." He raised his cup of coffee and took his time drinking, hopefully to end the questions from these gossiping old guys.

"Who was the stranger?" One asked. "I told you, it was a gun-slinger from Texas," another chimed in.

Stan, the owner and cook at the Woodsmen café came out of the kitchen then, to join the line-up of guys at the counter. His white apron held streaks of breakfast which he folded over as he sat. He listened to the talk, and then said, "Jesse, I'm sure I saw that foreigner last night. Well, this morning actually. I came in at 3AM to set some bread. Listen to this Jesse, I was outside having a smoke waiting for it to rise and I see this guy creeping close behind the buildings across from me. I thought to myself, you must have put on extra help for the week-end."

"No, I didn't. Did you see him up close? Would you recognize him again?" Jesse asked.

"The only thing I could make out was he was dressed in dark clothes." Stan offered shaking his head. "For a minute there, I did get the feeling that he was someone sneaking around."

Flo came out of the kitchen then laden with plates of eggs, crisp bacon and golden pancakes.

"Looks good," Reed said taking up his fork, "But after eating this I'll have to run at least four extra miles."

"Nah, eat and enjoy, I always say." The town's oldest resident offered. Somewhere in his nineties, today, Otto sat on his same stool at the counter drinking coffee after enjoying his eggs. He was dressed in his usual striped overalls, flannel shirt and sporting another of his many ties. His Old Spice aftershave lent a fragrant aroma to the room. Flo, the other oldest and respected female resident of town, buzzed around the café in her "nurse's shoes" in her important role as head waitress, and everyone knew she kept Stan's cafe going with a no nonsense training program. Her crepe soled shoes swished now as she refilled coffee cups. She had had her henna colored hair permed before the holiday week-end and just to make sure it looked good, she took a quick detour into the "biffy." She fluffed the hanky she always added to her uniform breast pocket and checked her nylons for runs, then puckered up her lips to make sure her lipstick hadn't run out into those fine lines that edged around her lips.

Flo didn't tell her age to anyone, and she wasn't even sure she knew because she had quit celebrating, but whatever, she liked her life, her job and who knows, maybe she'd let her guard down and one of these days get serious about a relationship. Now she made a run through the dining room with ice water and coffee and everyone seemed to be contentedly enjoying their breakfast.

Jesse's cell chirped in his pocket and after checking the number he took a breath. "Sheriff Montes," he answered.

"Jesse," the caller said, "this is Charlie MacGreger with the FBI. You called me?"

"Yup, it was me. You remember Birch Lake?" Jesse mopped his forehead with his paper napkin.

"Absolutely. What's up?"

"Charlie, I'm on my way into the office. Give me a minute and I'll call you back." Jesse clicked off his cell, reached in his pocket for some bills and laid them on the counter and took a last sip of his coffee.

Reed nodded at him and said "I'll catch up with you."

Thirty minutes later, he caught up with Jesse, who sat at his desk, still on the phone.

"Listen to this, Reed," Jesse said after finishing his call. "I faxed a description of Gunther Mueller, along with his prints and DNA to Charlie MacGreger, who is faxing it over to Scotland Yard."

"Good, they don't waste much time so we might hear something this morning even. You know, we'll have to call Daisy in." Reed mentioned then.

"God almighty, that's right," Jesse sat back and lit a cigar.

Reed shook his head. "Poor girl, she's overwhelmed with sadness after losing her best friend, and then, dreading the funeral tomorrow."

"Awful, just awful what this foreign ass-hole has done to my people," Jesse grumbled. "MacGreger is on the way here, and he'll be getting in around 8 PM tomorrow."

-29-

Daisy sucked in her breath when she saw the name Ron Randall in her appointment book. Ron had been Daisy's husband for seventeen years and now divorced; their two boys were grown and busy with their careers. Daisy had carefully planned her future after getting a hefty divorce settlement, and also a generous yearly maintenance that would go on indefinitely unless she remarried.

She put a hand under her chin as she sat and thought about the man. She had been in college when she met Ron. Tall, blond and handsome, Daisy had fallen for his charm and married the man after only a few months of dating. He had been just starting his career in medicine then and she quit college and went to work as a receptionist in his small office. Soon, however, she gave up her career when their two babies came along. Soon too, their married life began to fall apart as Doctor Randall spent less and less time at home as his medical reputation grew as he became known as a surgeon specializing in the cardiovascular field. Then one day, she accidentally ran into him with a woman and upon confronting them found out they were an item, well known around the medical arena. Deeply hurt and angry, after all the years when she had put him first, she found a well known divorce attorney. And several times over the years, the now famous Doctor Randall had tried to counter sue her, about having to shell out the tens of thousands of dollars she received yearly, but she would immediately send his complaints to her attorney, Reed Conners, who threatened to unleash some unfavorable comments to the masses if he persisted in harassing his client. That usually shut the man up, but Daisy wondered what he wanted now, or, if he had really come to Birch Lake for Roma's funeral. Knowing him well, Daisy couldn't imagine he didn't have another agenda.

Promptly at noon he walked in with not even a greeting. He remarked sarcastically, "So this is what you do with your time? I always knew you lacked ambition."

Daisy sucked in her breath. "Hello to you too," she replied. "What do you want, Ron?"

"I'm getting married for real this time and we're building a new home. So I won't be sending you anymore of my hard earned money. You can't rip me off any longer."

This was so like him to bring this up today, the day before Roma's funeral. "Get out, Ron," she whispered, "If you've got a complaint talk to Reed Conners."   And she walked to door and opened it saying, "Now leave or I'll call the Sheriff."

He spluttered, "Listen bitch, no hick small-town mouth-piece is going to tell me what to do!"

***

With a heavy heart, Daisy rushed back to the motel to get ready for Roma's funeral today. Her sons had wanted their mother buried in Birch Lake as this was where she had planned to live. But as Roma had not resided there yet, the townspeople agreed that a small token given to the church would forgive her absence and her sons had put a few thousand in the collection plate.

As Daisy got ready for the funeral, her hands shook as she applied her make-up. She dreaded this day. Roma's ex-husband would more than likely be there. She wondered if their ex's would be civil to each other. And the kids; Roma's and hers. Having grown up together, how would they all receive each other now? It was all so overwhelming.

The day before, Daisy had gone back to her house to get more of her things. As she ran through the rooms, she still got chills down her back as she scanned the corners for any more of the snakes.

Ed Harrison had tried time and again to ease her mind that her place was safe, but she just couldn't believe it. She still felt there were more of the critters hiding in the corners.

As she slipped into a black summer dress, she just couldn't believe she was getting ready to go to her friend's funeral and not out to a fun lunch with her. And now, the added stress of seeing all these people under these conditions gave her the jitters. Her own two boys were coming down from Minneapolis and would only be able to stay for several hours. She didn't know about Roma's family other then hearing that they were arriving that same day too. She jerked to attention when someone knocked at her door.

"Well Daisy Mae," Ed Harrison said as he stood in the doorway, "I thought I'd see if you needed a hand. If you've got other plans, that's okay." He was dressed in a blue suit.

She took his arm and pulled him into her room. "Oh, my God Ed, thanks. I'm worrying about how to get through this."

"That's what I thought. I'll be there to help you if you want." And he was at her side all through the day.

When she saw her two sons enter the church with their father, she motioned them to join her in the pew. She stood up for their hugs and settled them next to her in the seats. She ignored her ex, who followed them. When Roma's family came into the church following the casket, Daisy put her hand over her lips to cover her outcry. Ed put a hand over hers to steady her, and then the service began.

A short time later, at the cemetery as they lowered Roma into the ground, Daisy felt as though her heart would stop with the heavy load of grief she was feeling. Finally turning away, she hung on to her son's hands for dear life as they went over to Roma's family, where she hugged Roma's grown sons. Other then saying how sorry they all were, there wasn't much else to say at this time so they stood silently for a few moments then nodded respectfully and moved on. Then finally it was over. She had hugged her son's again and they had promised to come back in several weeks for a real visit, and she saw them get in their dad's Mercedes to catch a ride back to Minneapolis.

And now, it was over. She hiccupped as Ed helped her into his car. "Would you like to come to my house and have some wine and relax?" He leaned in and asked.

Daisy was silent. After the hullabaloo of the last few weeks, it was finally over. She'd killed a man, three people were dead, her house was unlivable and she was homeless. It didn't take her long to accept the invitation for his company.

Now looking like a picture right out of House Beautiful, she saw Ed Harrison's home was a red brick and stucco that encompassed approximately three thousand square feet of living space. Landscaped with an emerald green lawn with shrubs and flower beds, not one single weed poked its mangy head out to spoil the view. This afternoon was the first time Daisy had taken a really good look at his environment and even in her exhausted state, she was impressed with his taste in up-scale living. Of course she remembered that growing up, the Harrison family had been affluent auto dealers and when they retired and Ed had taken over the business, both parents had died shortly after. She also remembered the gossip when he had torn down the old family home and built this eye catcher.

As they sat outside under the shaded terrace, sipping glasses of wine, the evening sun glistened off the pool.

"Want to take a dip?" he asked. "There are some suits in the pool-house that would fit you I'm sure. Daisy, I think it would help you relax."

Daisy leaned her head back against the chaise and closed her eyes, as the events of these several weeks filed through her thoughts like a moving picture show again. Would they ever stop? She murmured under her breath. Then sitting up, she made up her mind.

"Thank you, Ed," she said, "this is exactly what I need. Now where do I find that bathing suit?"

-30-

Sheriff Jesse Montes hung his cap on the rack and settled at his desk. He and his wife had attended the funeral the day before for Roma Hurst. Not that they were acquainted with the deceased, but out of respect for Daisy O'Dell whom they knew well. Of course the whole town was there too, even though they didn't know the woman either, but this was a big event.

As Jesse opened his mail and answered his telephone calls, the morning flew by and just as he took a minute and sat back, FBI Agent Tom MacGreger strolled into his office after parking his black SUV rental.

"Hey buddy," Jesse greeted him. "You got good connections, I see." He got up and extended his hand to MacGreger.

"Not bad. I left Virginia at four AM." The FBI agent commented as they shook hands.

"I'm glad you could come back on such short notice." Jesse said. "Take a seat, I just made some fresh coffee. Can I fix a cup for you?"

"Man that sounds good, the stuff they give you on the plane is awful." Tom MacGreger grumbled. The agent did not wear the usual blue suit and white shirt but was dressed casually in brown slacks, brown t-shirt and a tan sport coat. His auburn tousled curly hair and brown eyes matched his attire. He sat his six foot stocky frame down and put a foot over his other knee.

"Hey, thanks for calling me Jesse. I was just about to take some vacation time so you caught me at a good time." He drank some of his coffee and took out a cigarette. "Okay, if I smoke?"

"Yep, and I'll join you," Jesse remarked. After the two men got comfortable with their vices, Jesse went on. "Let me start at the beginning and bring you up on my dilemma. Listen to this, it all started when one of our residents got a visit from her friend, who came here from Norway." And he went on to describe Roma's arrival, her relationship with Gunther Mueller, and the trouble he thrust on her and then ultimately, how all this effected Daisy. He ended by saying, "Now I've got both a dead woman and a dead man in the morgue and I need to find out who these people are."

Agent MacGreger listened attentively as Jesse gave him the details; then MacGreger went on, "Jesse, after we talked, I contacted both Interpol and Scotland Yard with Mueller's description." Then added, "I've not heard back from my man as yet, as I told him I would be traveling until noon today."

"From what the deceased Roma Hurst told us, the man lived in Oslo. But of course that doesn't mean he was a born citizen of that country." Jesse said and sat back in his chair which creaked plaintively from his weight. He went on, "She did tell Daisy that he often disappeared, and he would be gone for weeks without an explanation."

MacGreger nodded. "Did he ever admit to being a gun for hire?"

Jesse shook his head. "She said when she confronted him with what she'd heard, and that she was going to leave him and Norway, he threatened to kill her if she tried to get away from him."

"Tell me how she got this far?" MacGreger asked.

Jesse laughed, "That woman had balls. She got away from him at the airport over there, and then hid out for a few weeks after she got here. I guess when she finally showed up at Daisy's shop, she was disguised as an old lady."

MacGreger blew a smoke ring as he tilted the straight chair back. "So when did this killer surface?" He asked.

"Listen to this, he sent a woman first to front for him and she must have slipped the snakes in Roma's luggage sometime at the airport. When Roma first opened her suitcases at Daisy's house these two poisonous ones crawled out and got loose in Daisy's house."

"Jesus," MacGreger managed to say. "Who was the woman?"

"So far I don't know that either. But she got hers when she was bitten by one of those reptiles. Now I've got her on ice over at the funeral home. I've put out notices with sheriff's departments all over the country, but no one has come forward here."

"She's probable from over-seas too. I can send out inquiries for you."

Jesse blew out a cloud of smoke. "Thanks, that would help."

"So when did this Gunther Mueller show his face?" MacGreger asked.

"The first and only time I saw him was a few days before the funeral. He was dead. That day he had killed Roma, but that night he got his. We had the Sheriff Departments from surrounding towns helping us but the fucker met his maker at the business end of Daisy's gun. He had broken through our line of men guarding her at Ed Harrison's and found her. She blasted him and practically blew his head off just before he got a chance to kill her using a ligature again."

MacGreger grimaced. "The famous silent killer. Well known and used amongst assassins, because they don't have to carry around much heavy artillery."

"God almighty, he just about got her too." Jesse drank the last of his coffee.

"Just how did she get him?" Tom MacGreger asked curiously.

"She was staying over at Ed's house, a local who was keeping an eye on her. Even though we had a number of law men watching his place, Mueller managed to get in the house. Daisy said sometime in the early morning after lying awake all night in a guest bedroom, she felt a presence in the house, and then hid. And sure enough without a sound he appeared at her bedside, and as he bent to slip this looped wire over her head she blasted him." Jesse wiped his brow.

"Jesus, lucky she was awake." Just then MacGreger's cell phone vibrated in his pocket. "Tom MacGreger," he said into it, then got up and paced and then gave Jesse the high sign as he listened, and after a few minutes hung up.

"Okay," he said coming back and sitting down. "Scotland Yard says they have a possible match for Mueller, but they need DNA to be sure. And Oslo PD has a missing person alert for a woman who matches the description who vanished months ago. They want DNA as well."

"Now we're getting somewhere. Let's go see the coroner and help him send those off." And the two men left the deputy and the new intern to man the Birch Lake phones in the sheriff's office. "If you need me, call me on my cell," Jesse instructed them.

After taking care of that task over at the funeral home with the coroner/medical examiner/ funeral director, the two men stopped in at the Legion, the local gathering place for something cold for their parched throats. Heads turned at their arrival as they took stools at the bar. Jesse ordered a diet coke and MacGreger did the same. This evening, Otto and Flo were sitting next to each other on stools, deep in conversation. When Judy, the bartender brought Jesse and Tom's drinks over, she asked unabashed, always on the look-out for a new boyfriend, "Who's your friend, Jesse?" Then smiled waiting for the introduction.

***

The next day bright and early, Tom MacGreger met Jesse at the sheriff's office in downtown Birch Lake again. "I figure I should be hearing from Scotland Yard or Interpol this morning, so I wanted to be here when the calls come through."

"Thanks Tom. I stopped and picked up some rolls. And the coffee is just done." Jesse poured two cups of the strong caffeine and the two men enjoyed the fresh tasty apple turnovers just out of the oven from the bakery down the street.

When MacGreger's cell phone rang minutes later, he picked up and raised a thumb in the air to let Jesse know it was the call they had been waiting for. And after listening intently for minutes he thanked the caller and hung up.

"Okay, here's what they have. You'll remember this from the news years ago Jesse. The kidnappers were never caught and the case was never solved. DNA was found and it matched a fifty year old male, citizenship unknown, believed to be involved in the 2005 kidnapping of this Princess Rosa of that small town in Italy? It went on for weeks and finally a huge ransom was paid, but in the end the princess was dead." MacGreger lit a cigarette.

"God almighty, no wonder Roma was afraid of this man!" Jesse remarked. "Did you get a name?"

"The same, Gunther Mueller, they say, but no known address, or family."

Jesse was silent for a minute. "What the hell am I supposed to do with his body?"

"They're still working on it. But wait a minute. We have good news on the woman. The DNA matched and her name is Astrid Wold. Her family lives in Bergen, Norway and they will pay to have her body sent back there for burial."

"Well, thank God," Jesse said. "I'll give a call to the funeral home. They'll be glad to hear that. Out of curiosity Tom, I wonder how long I'm obliged to keep a body on ice, by chance do you know?"

"Hmm-, that's something you and departments across the pond will have to come to an agreement on."

"Oh crap," Jesse mumbled under his breath, "I don't have that much time left in office to get into all this now!"

-31-

"Thanks Ed, for all you've done for me," Daisy said climbing out of the shiny black SUV. "I'm sure I would not be here now, otherwise." He had given her a ride back to the 59 Motel in Birch Lake where she was staying, even though her house had been fumigated and proclaimed free of any marauders by the Bug Company, and painstakingly searched by Ed.

He got out of the SUV and went around to give her a hand in getting down. "Daisy, why don't you pick up some things and come back with me. Stay for a few days." He said as she got her key to her room out of her purse.

She stood still at the door and thought about that. After her swim in his pool, she'd swept her wet silver hair up off her face and reapplied her make-up. And feeling better than she had for days after the meal he'd fixed, and then still somewhat tipsy after the wine, it did sound inviting to have him want to take care of her longer.

"Why don't you close your shop and we could go out and stay on the lake." Ed insisted again taking her room key and opening the door, then standing aside as she entered.

After thinking about his invitation and then remembering how her body had responded to his embrace earlier, she didn't know which way to reply to his invitation. If she agreed to go with him, surely a romantic liaison would begin. And, was she ready to go there?

Ed waited for her answer as they stood inside her doorway. "Thank you for everything you've done for me," she said finally, "but I've got to say no to your invitation. It sounds wonderful but I need some time."

Disappointment crossed Ed's handsome face. "But Daisy, you shouldn't be alone," he persisted.

Daisy swept a hand over her forehead, where a headache was starting to ripple though her head. For God's sake, she just needed to lie down and be quiet. She turned to him and hugged him quickly and then shut the door.

Inside her motel room, she kicked off her wedgies, tossed her clothes over a chair and slid between the sheets. It was only seven o'clock in the evening. Maybe a good night of sleep would give her thoughts a rest from all the sorrowful events going through her mind. Then just to make sure she got back up and found the bottle of aspirin in her suitcase and swallowed two, without water. Then, finally she slept soundly through the night and awoke early in the morning as a garbage truck rumbled through downtown Birch and screeched its brakes as it stopped close by.

Daisy turned on her side in the bed, and for a few minutes she was at a loss as to where she was. Why wasn't she in her own king-size bed at home? Then it all came flooding back, especially killing that man. And then the picture of what that gunshot had done to the person.

Well, to hell with you Gunther Mueller, you got what you deserved, Daisy said to the walls. Then she tossed her covers off and stood up, determined to get motivated. First of all, she was going home. But still somewhat nervous about the safety of it, an idea had come to her in her sleep. She'd get a dog to police her house. She'd seen it on the internet. Certain kinds of dogs could be trained to warn its owners of danger. Well, maybe she'd call Ed and run the idea past him. He seemed pretty informed and resourceful. And after showering and getting ready for work, she called him and told him of her idea.

"Daisy Mae," he greeted her, "I know where you can get just such an animal," he remarked. "I'm in my

Hummer right now on my way over to my office, but I'll make some calls. I guarantee you'll love this."

At the end of her busy day of doing acrylic nails, manicures and pedicures, Daisy was totally wiped and hurried to tidy her shop when Ed breezed in with a leash in his hand.

"Daisy, meet your new room-mate. This is Romeo!" And Daisy looked down at her feet and saw what looked like a pile of rags. When it started licking her ankles, she bent down to get a better look.

"My God, it's a dog!" She joked and stroked his raggedy fur.

"Yes my dear, this little spitfire will tear anything that slithers into a million pieces. I guarantee he won't let even a mouse take up residence in your house!"

"How do you know that?" Daisy asked, kneeling and rubbing the dog's stomach.

"The kennel owner and trainer showed me an example of his qualities. Within a nanosecond this little shit had a snake torn to bits."

Daisy looked doubtful.

"Come on, I'll follow you home and bring him in to your house," Ed went on, "We'll see what he does."

At her house, Daisy unlocked the door and Ed let Romeo out of his kennel and the little pile of rags immediately went off to explore.

"Okay, if I make some coffee? Let's see what he does," Ed said as they came into the kitchen.

Daisy set her suitcase down and went right to one of the stools at the counter and put her feet up on a rung. She looked around uneasily.

Soon the coffee was done and as Daisy and Ed sat at the counter in the kitchen, they heard a snuffling going on and soon Romeo came back in the kitchen and dropped a dead mouse at Daisy's feet. And in the course of a couple of hours, he had brought her gifts of two more, also a squirming June bug and a huge moth.

"The trainer said, this small animal is trained to not stop hunting until you say, "stop" and clap her hands."

"Okay, but how will I know when this house is safe?" Daisy asked still worried.

Ed looked sorrowful, "I can't answer that for sure, Daisy, but why don't we leave Romeo here for awhile longer and go out and get a bite to eat and come back and see what he has captured."

As tired as Daisy felt, this sounded like a good idea. The longer this small dynamo had in there the better she felt. So they went the few miles to the casino in the next town and ate a sumptuous meal.

Tonight the feature was garlic-infused Angus farm raised prime rib that melted in your mouth. Baked yellow Yukon potatoes with a creamy parmesan sauce, and fresh asparagus with a hollandaise pottage.

"My gosh, if I ate like this too many times, I'd be waddling like a duck." Daisy laughed for the first time in days and it felt good. Too many things had saddened her lately and taken away her usual zest for life. For the first time now she began to feel like her old self on the ride back to Birch Lake.

At her house, Ed went in first and called for Romeo. As they came into the kitchen in the same place on the floor he had dropped his gifts earlier, now he stood proudly before his next presents. Bending closer they saw another mouse, a good sized black spider and a big dust ball.

"Well, see your new houseguest has been busy." And Ed picked up the gifts with a paper towel and went out to the garbage can. Coming back inside he asked, "Do you feel any safer now, Daisy?"

By now Daisy did, and she bent down to stroke her new pet's head. "Okay Romeo my boy, you can stay but you have to keep an eye out for me." And he licked her hands and even seemed to smile at her. So she had a guest in her house after all.

Several days later, Daisy remembered she had Roma's makeup bag. She had tossed Roma's scattered pots and jars together at the motel after her death and had brought it back when she'd come home. Now the large leopard print bag stood forlornly in the room which was bare of any other of Roma's belongings, as she had tossed her suitcases and all her clothes in the garbage when she had first found the snakes that had lived amongst them.

Daisy laid out her things on the top of a dresser in the guest room. There were lotions and wrinkle creams, moisture and oil-free. When she opened one jar of cream the scent was of heavenly purple lilacs. Her eye-makeup was a mixture of dark and luminous for nighttime and cool blue and greens for day. When Daisy took out a crystal bottle of cologne, and spritzed some in the air, she recognized Prada, the fragrance that Roma always wore. She had to sit down on the edge of the guest bed for a moment then. Was she really gone? She asked herself again and then she wiped her eyes. She would have to box all these personal things up and find out where her sons lived and mail it to them.

Then as she got to the bottom of the make-up bag, Daisy found a letter that was addressed to her. It was sealed and had her full name, Daisy O'Dell, written plainly on the front of the envelope. She sat back down on the bed again and in shaking hands tore open the letter. At first it didn't register just what Roma had written. It read like this-

My dearest friend Daisy; If, this letter falls into your hands it will mean I am dead. Intuition tells me Gunther will find me and he will not let me live.

The letter went on-

My boys are fixed for life with assets from their father's inventions and they don't need any more money as they will inherit from their dad when he succumbs. Daisy, I've loved having you as my best friend and now I want you to enjoy all my glorious wealth, so I'm leaving all my earthly assets to you. And there were notarized papers with Roma's instructions carefully laid out. PS; She had added, Bring these to your attorney promptly.

Daisy sat immobilized in unbelief. Roma had given her all of her belongings!

She shook her head but unable to think further, she stood up and numbly returned the bottles and jars to Roma's make-up bag. Then she went back to the kitchen with Romeo snuffling at her heels and cried some more.

-32-

Daisy awoke with a start the next morning. Something astounding in the back recesses of her mind had abruptly awakened her. She turned over to her side and waited sleepily for it to surface. No need to rush, she thought seeing the last vestiges of darkness in the room. Soon the sun would be up and then she had several hours, plenty of time to get ready for work.

She lazily stretched and yawned, and then suddenly remembered finding Roma's letter to her the day before. The letter she'd read over and over into the night.

I have to call Reed, she exclaimed and in her haste to get out of bed, she distractedly looked around in alarm for the reason there was so much bustling going on under her bed linens. Then she remembered Romeo, and saw the little brown and black mess of flying fur. She watched as he clattered to the hard wood floor, slipped and rolled over a few times, then caught up to her heels in a run.

"Romeo, I forgot all about you," Daisy said to her new pet. "Well, come on then, I better let you outside," and they both hurried to the back door.

"Hurry up," Daisy said as he ran around in circles and then rushed right over to a pot of geraniums and relieved himself. She could swear he smiled at her for praise, then rushed over and licked her ankles. "You little shit; you better not do that again!" And after gulping every bit of his breakfast with relish, Daisy said, "now my friend, it's time for you to get to work, go on now." And, Romeo put his nose to the floor and busily scampered off.

She put the coffee on and then picked up the phone and dialed Reed Conners.

"Good morning Reed, this is Daisy. Is it too early for a call?" She asked.

"Nope, I'm up." Reed said. "What's going on?"

"I wonder if I could see you. I've got some important papers I need you to look at."

"Sure, come on over. Does nine work?" He asked.

With that done Daisy hurried to the shower, put on her make-up, then dressed in a pink running suit and grabbed her papers and purse. Then she remembered Romeo, just as she was about to get in her car. Running back into the kitchen she refilled his water and put some snacks in his other bowl, and told him to "watch the house and keep hunting."

Reed lived three miles out of Birch Lake right on the water on the opposite side of the town. As she turned off highway #371 onto his private road that led through woods, the maple trees were ablaze in reds and gold, a sharp contrast to the emerald green of the assorted pines, which perfumed the morning air with their earthy green aroma. Entering Reed's yard, she had forgotten how beautiful his landscaped peninsula was. The white bark on the birch trees glistened and the coin like leaves cast long shadows across the lawn.

Daisy got out of her Porsche and gazed around as she walked up to the door.

"Come on in," Reed said, apparently watching for her and opening it.

Daisy greeted him. "Thanks for seeing me. Reed, it's so beautiful here!"

"Thanks," he said. "I like it too. Best thing I ever did was sell my ranch, retire and move here and remodel this old place."

"That's right. This has been in your family for years, hasn't it?" Daisy remarked.

"My folks bought it way back when I was a kid," Reed said as he led her into the kitchen. "Here, have a seat while I'll get the coffee. Oh, you remember

Lindy, don't you?" He asked as Lindy came into the kitchen.

Daisy smiled at Lindy. Of course, they had met time and again over the years and Daisy greeted her now. "Good to see you Lindy." She was about to go on and ask, "Are you staying long?" when she caught herself just in the nick of time. She'd heard the townsfolk felt this woman took unfair advantage of one of their own, but of course everyone loved Reed and wouldn't say that to him for the world.

Lindy Lewis reached for a cup in the cupboard. Her blond hair was in a short pony tail and her attire consisted of skimpy shorts, halter and flip flops. "Hello Daisy," she said smiling at her, then added, "I'm sorry about all your bad luck."

"Thank you Lindy," Daisy said politely. "Now I know what you went through when all those people from across the border were after you!"

"Oh Lordy, don't remind me." Lindy picked up her cup of coffee which Reed had poured for her. "I'm going out to get some sun, so please excuse me." She said then and went out to sit on the dock.

"Come on to my office, Daisy," Reed said and after they had made small talk for a few minutes, Daisy took the papers out of her purse.

"Here's what I needed to see you about, Reed. I'm not sure how to take this. If these are legal or what." And she handed him the papers Roma had left for her.

Reed was quiet while he studied them, and to occupy her jumbled mind Daisy looked around his office. Three walls were filled with books; there were paperbacks in one section, then hard-cover in another. When she looked closer she saw one whole shelf was filled with John Macdonald's mysteries. She sat back in her leather chair and took a deep breath. The faint aroma of tobacco mixed with the rich smell of the leather was pleasant.

Reed whistled as he finally put down the papers. "Daisy, according to these papers you might be a very rich lady! From what I've heard, Roma was financially well off. "

Daisy looked at him and just shook her head.

"Daisy, believe me. These papers are legal!" He sat back in his leather chair and went on, "You will need to see an estate attorney first and find out how to proceed. I assume all her holdings are in Norway. Or, maybe since she was relocating here, she has already made the transfers to one of our banking institutions."

Daisy swallowed, her throat and mouth were parched and she hurriedly took another drink of her coffee. "I have no idea, what she might have done. You know, before," and she swallowed hard to ward off tears, "before she died, we just didn't have much time with so many things going on."

"I can make some calls for you Daisy. I know an estate attorney in Minneapolis who specializes in "sudden wealth."   And you'll also need to find a financial advisor and a CPA that you absolutely trust."

"Reed, if you could set me up with this attorney in the twin cities, would you consider coming along with me?" Daisy asked nervously.

"I'd be glad too," he volunteered.

"You can bill me, Reed, to include everything," Daisy said. She looked at him again, her eyes sad. "I have a hard time believing all this," she said again.

Reed ran a hand through his hair and brushed it off his forehead. "These papers are good, Daisy. Why don't I call my friend in Minneapolis and see what he's got to say."

"Thank you Reed, anything you can do." She smiled for the first time that morning, and then listened to his end of the conversation.

After making connections and greetings, Reed explained what he needed. That a good friend had papers inheriting what might be a goodly amount. He asked for a date for them to come in. When the very next day was open in the morning, he asked Daisy if she could make it. She nodded her head in the affirmative. "Okay buddy, we'll see you in the AM." Reed closed his cell.

"Wow, that was fast," Daisy whispered. "Okay, what should I bring along besides these papers?"

"I would say your usual; driver's license, social security card and for some reason I think you should have your passport available. Don't be surprised if you might have to make a fast trip to Norway soon too".

Daisy stood up, her thoughts still in a whirl. "Okay, I can meet you here tomorrow. How early should we leave?"

Reed stood too and they walked to the front door. "How about six? Then we'll have time to get some breakfast, and meet at the attorney's office at 10:00."

Daisy rushed back to Birch, checked on Romeo, and then opened her shop. The day was packed with the usual repair work, and a number of new appointments wanting the complete sets of acrylic nails. These were good money makers which she liked because it promised the need of further services. Then she got on the phone and changed her appointments for the following day, cramming them into evenings and earlier in the mornings to catch up.

Actually she was so busy the day flew by and when she got home, and opened the front door, she could hear Romeo's nails clacking on the wood floor as he scrambled to meet her. Then in a flurry he rushed by and lifted his leg on another pot of flowers blooming profusely on her porch.

"Oh for God's sake," she yelled at the miniature dog, "You will kill all my flowers!" He looked at her with hurt in his brown eyes. Feeling bad for yelling at him, she bent down and patted his head. Now she supposed he didn't know what to make of her actions.

Coming into the kitchen then, in the same spot where he had brought her gifts earlier was something that absolutely made her yell again! Pieces of snake skin lay in a nice little pile on the same spot he had declared his gifting area. And now, her feeling of safety she thought she had gained with Romeo's visit vanished. There were more snakes in her house!

She dared to step closer and stared at the chewed up pieces of snakeskin. Wait, something about it looked familiar. When something shiny and silver lay off to the side caught her eye, she realized it was the buckle to the snakeskin belt that went with her new outfit. The belt must have fallen down on the closet floor.

"Romeo, bad dog," she exclaimed and shook a finger at him as she scooped up the tangled mess. Romeo stood off to the side and watched with apprehensive eyes.

"Well buddy," Daisy said, "we're going to need to have that serious talk." But she remembered he needed his supper and filled his dish with goodies and set it on the floor for him. Romeo didn't move but looked at his yummy dinner, then at her with those big brown sad eyes.

"Oh for God's sake," Daisy repeated tiredly. She bent down realizing he was probably waiting for permission to eat. "It's okay," she murmured and stroked his head. Then he bustled over and began chomping hungrily.

She laid out a lime green linen a-line dress for the trip down to Minneapolis the next morning with Reed. But she slept poorly that night, as her dreams were still vivid with the violent shooting scenes.

"I've got a thermos of coffee and some brownies Lindy made for our trip." Reed greeted her the next morning as she rang his doorbell at six. He was dressed in pressed jeans, a white shirt cuffed at the wrist and carried a blue cashmere sport coat on a hanger.

"That sounds wonderful," Daisy said. "I didn't have time to even start the coffee this morning since my new roommate came to stay," she added dryly.

"You got company?" he asked as they had settled in his Corvette and sped through his colorful woods to highway #371.

"If you can call a dog company. He's a small black and brown bundle of what looks like a pile of rags."

Reed laughed. "Yeah?"

Daisy went on, "It's a long story. He was a gift."

"I see. What kind of dog is it? Reed asked.

"I don't have any idea," Daisy remarked, "but listen to this, he's a snake hunter!"

"I've read how certain breeds of dogs can be trained for that. They're popular in states like Arizona and Florida."

"Really, I guess I've never thought about it before," and they rode in silence for awhile. Then

Reed asked, "Have you thought what you are going to do with this money when you get it, Daisy?"

Daisy just rolled her eyes and shook her head.

-33-

After bringing Romeo to a kennel for the day earlier, the three hour drive down to Minneapolis flew by as Daisy and Reed talked mostly about old times. Daisy had grown up in Birch Lake as her parents had been shop keepers in those years and ran the local grocery store. She had spent all her summers helping her folks and brothers as they also sold fertilizers, feeds and seeds. When she got older and protested doing man's work, her dad allowed her to work in the office. Here she learned how to keep the company's books, but as soon as she graduated from high school, she packed her new set of luggage and boarded the Greyhound for Minneapolis and college. Here she studied her love of interior design and soon went to work.

"Did you start your own design business?" Reed asked her now.

"I wanted to, but then I met the infamous doctor and we got married. I had only meant to help him out in his new office for a short time, to get him started. But then I got pregnant and foolishly gave up all my own plans for him."

"Too bad, Daisy," Reed said, "So you worked for him and then stayed home and had babies."

"Don't get me wrong. I loved it for many years but when the boys got into high school I had more time. And that's when it dawned on me my marriage was in trouble. That's when I found out he had another life going on with somebody else."

"You divorced him then."

"Oh boy did I!" Daisy remarked with emphasis. "Here, I had given up almost twenty good years of my life for him totally, and then he'd been spending his time in bed with someone else!"

"I'm sorry to hear that." Reed shifted lanes to get out of the way for a semi as he talked.

"Well, you know there's nothing like a woman scorned and I got even. I found the best divorce attorney in Minneapolis and took him for almost every last dollar he made, and then, I also got a court order for maintenance forever!"

"He came to see me when he was here a few days ago." Reed said.

"I thought he would." Daisy remarked and then added, "The jerk came into my shop too and told me he was getting married again, for real this time. That they were building a new house and he wouldn't be sending me any more money."

Reed shook his head. "He was grumbling about how much of his hard earned money he had to part with each month for you. I advised him to live with it."

"Poor guy." Daisy laughed. "Please can we stop soon for a smoke?" she asked.

"Sure, I was thinking the same thing. There's a rest-stop up here shortly." And within minutes Reed swung into area. After restroom breaks, they got sodas and enjoyed the brownies, and their smokes at a picnic table in the shade of a huge oak tree.

As they passed by the huge casino in Milaca, Daisy remembered the times back in those early years, when she and her husband had gone there for a week-end. Which they would mostly spend in bed, she recalled, shaking her head.

Then she asked, "Reed, how come you've never married?"

"Just didn't take the time, I guess," he said under his breath.

"Well, marriage isn't everything. But you should have kids. There's nothing like the love of them."

"Hmm-," was all Reed said.

They rode in silence for awhile then, and soon they were caught up in the heavy early morning Minneapolis traffic as the masses made their way into the city for their day of trade. After parking in a ramp downtown, they made their way to Peter's Grill, an old standby they were both familiar with.

Miller, Johns and Evans was the name of the legal offices they entered shortly before ten o'clock. Daisy had reapplied her lipstick and now wet her lips nervously as they were told to have a seat, and that Mr. Miller would be available shortly.

A picture of calm, Reed sat next to her in an easy chair and put a foot over a knee. Looking at him, Daisy wondered if he ever got nervous about anything. In his business as a fraud investigator for a huge insurance company here in the city, he'd talked about some close calls he'd had over the years. But never anything so nerve-wracking he'd want to give up the work. After a short wait, they were ushered in to meet Mr. Miller.

"Hello Reed. Good to see you again." Mr. Miller exclaimed, extending his hand.

Reed greeted him and shook hands and then introduced Daisy.

"This is the friend from Birch Lake whom we spoke off last night," He said. And Daisy stepped up and smiled.

"My friends call me Billy," he said. "Come on in and sit down."

Billy Miller's office was on the top floor of a building some forty stories up. Daisy had always been nervous about heights and now her heart was in her throat, not only about this whole awesome turn of events, but now she had to worry about getting back down the forty stories and not fainting from fright in the interim.

As Billy Miller was busy instructing his secretary to fetch some coffee, Daisy glanced around his luxurious, contemporary furnished office. As a schooled designer herself, and although she had never worked in the industry, she recognized all of it had been done by the expertise of an upscale interior designer. The first thing she'd felt as they stepped in the suite of offices was the cool dry air, and then inhaled the pleasant scent. A combination of pine forests with a trace of an expensive fragrance, she thought with a smile. The floor was a dark stained oak and the color scheme was assorted shades of green. Persian rugs anchored a sitting area with matching figured damask couches with solid colored easy chairs. Off to the side a large conference table of gleaming dark mahogany stood with a dozen cushioned chairs in the large room. Expensive modern art decorated walls, and beautiful accessories adorned the tops of tables. The breathtaking view looked out at neighboring skyscrapers and across the city onto the suburbs and lakes. Soft classical music played in the background and nostalgia rippled through Daisy's stomach now as she found Plymouth, her old suburb far off in the distance, silhouetted against a backdrop of grown trees and added roads.

This all took just a minute of her time before she sat down in one of the soft chairs in front of Billy Miller's desk. Reed took the matching one.

"It's a pleasure to make your acquaintance, Miss O'Dell. I understand you used to live here in the city?" The attorney asked then.

Daisy swallowed over her nerves. "I did," she said. "I moved here for college then stayed on. I married a doctor and raised two sons here."

"What made you decide to move to Birch Lake?" Billy Miller asked.

"Birch is my home town. After I got a divorce, I decided I wanted to slow down the pace of my life."

"And did it happen?" He smiled.

"Absolutely," Daisy said, more relaxed now, then added warily, "Or it did until all these things started happening just weeks ago."

Just then a secretary came in carrying a tray and for a few minutes everyone was tantalized by the tempting essences of the cinnamon Danish and fresh brewed coffee. And while they ate, Billy Miller asked Daisy how and when she had gotten to know Roma Hurst and she told of the time they had met over their back-yard fences, as their youngsters played in their sand-boxes and toys. How they had become close friends through the years and then how their lives began to fall apart as the kids got older.

Reed cleared his throat and stepped in. "Billy," he said then, "I'm sure you read of the trouble we had in Birch several weeks ago when this unscrupulous character came to town from Europe and caused so much havoc. We had three deaths."

Billy Miller nodded. "I read about it with concern, and I've got to say for a small town you sure have had a lot of excitement this summer."

Reed inhaled. "I'm sure we will all think of it as the horrible summer of 2012. Normally the most excitement we have is when a carload of beer-sodden fishermen stop in at the Legion." They all laughed.

"I understand you were forced to shoot this Gunther Meuller, Daisy?" Billy asked.

Daisy sucked in her breath. "He killed Roma, my best friend and he would have gotten me too. I had no choice."

"Terrible situation. Now, Reed told me that you found a note from her saying that she was leaving all her holdings to you."

Daisy reached in her purse and took out the paper which she had put in a clear plastic cover. "I was gathering up her things and found this."

Billy Miller was silent as he studied the paper. "Well, now the first thing I have to do is make a copy of this, then I suggest you put this away in a safe deposit box immediately." He handed the paper back to her. "Then I need to get a copy of her death certificate, and we'll proceed from there."

Daisy took a deep breath to steady her voice. "I brought that. And I also brought along a folder she had in her suitcase. I haven't gone through any of it as I didn't want to go through her personal papers."

Billy Miller smiled and reached out for it. "That makes this a lot easier. Let's see what she has here." He studied each paper and laid them out on his desk. And after minutes he added, "Your friend kept meticulous records. I see she has transferred a large amount of capital to a financial house here in Minneapolis. Hmm-, then I see she has an account in the Caymans."

"Really," Daisy whispered and sat immobilized. "What on earth should I do?" She continued to herself.

"Well, I'd advise you to count your lucky stars, Miss O'Dell." He said and smiled. "Of course, I will have to do extensive investigating on your behalf. She mentioned in her will that her children had sizable trusts and funds set up by their father, but I must warn you, do not think for a minute that they won't want her riches as well."

Daisy looked crestfallen. "Of course, it would only be right!" She said then.

"But, we will proceed with her wishes," Miller said then. "Now, if you two would like to go out to lunch, and give me some time, I will have the necessary papers drawn up for you ready to sign in several hours."

Reed stood up, as Daisy gathered her purse. "Thank you Mr. Miller," she said frowning slightly. At this point she didn't know how to feel. Should she be anxious fearing Roma's sons would claim their right to their mother's estate? Or were they so well established they would gladly share the wealth. E.B. Hurst, world renowned inventor of numerous medical devices, their father and Roma's ex, was a multi-millionaire known worldwide for his inventions in the medical field.

Daisy stood up and smoothed her linen dress. For God's sake, she thought to herself as they walked out of Millers office. I don't need Roma's money and I don't know if I want to go on with this. Reed noticed the look on her face as they got in the elevator.

"What's wrong?" He asked as they began to descend the forty floors.

Nervously clinging to the hold bars in the enclosed elevator, Daisy murmured under her breath. "Maybe I shouldn't proceed with this Reed. Maybe Roma wasn't serious and it's all some kind of a joke."

Reed cleared his throat and swiped a hand through his hair. "You know Daisy, when a person signs his name to a declaration made in his own handwriting to a paper, the court sees it as a legal document."

Daisy could only shake her head in confusion. And if she had known then what she was getting into, she would have run, very fast, from pursuing this venture any further.

-34-

In a coffee shop in Oslo two men sat with their heads together deep in a hushed conversation and exchanged the ill-gotten news. In their business, normally their actual line of employment was never acknowledged or discussed openly but today the assassins were horrified at the leak in the structure of their world and overruled the practice.

"They said it was a fuck-up. Astrid was killed too." Bjorn whispered and Axel, who sat across from him, quickly moved back and waved a hand in the air.

"Jesus, Bjorn get some soap. Your breath stinks like rotten fish!" Axel mumbled.

"Yeah?" Bjorn didn't take the bloke seriously. "Listen bugger," he said. "Here's what our cousin, that there ghoul in that place called Birch said. 'Some woman they call Daisy killed Gunther'."

Axel drank his coffee in silence and let the bloke blather on.

"Why don't you come in with me and we plan a trip over to the US," Bjorn asked then. "The caller said that Gunther's old lady gave all her penga to this Daisy. And you can be sure old Gunther had a fortune on himself too."

"Why do you care Bjorn, you don't need the money. You're not poor," Axel commented dryly.

"Fuck, Axel, one never has enough. Come along and we can see the country, and take care of business."

"Nah, you go. I'll keep an ear out for you." And Axel contentedly slurped his dark roast coffee.

Bjorn Olafson was called a self-absorbed bigoted recluse. He didn't have any friends and lived by himself; in a modern condominium in the affluent Oslo neighborhood that border lined the fjords by the ocean. As a man in his prime, at forty five years of age, he lived life to the hilt. He was considered handsome with his golden blond hair and piercing blue eyes and his muscle bound body was always clad in expensive clothes. He had a mistress whom he would spend an occasional night with, but he had a quirk as he never took his clothes off in her presence, not even when they had sex. He had a horror of letting anyone see him naked, and that was because he had a very hairy body. Covered in a golden hair suit, he had sought out the best doctors in Europe, but to his chagrin found it was only an abnormal malady caused by over-active hair follicles in his skin. In his younger years he had tried numerous methods to rid himself of this horror with countless creams and potions, but to no avail, as it grew back faster and thicker than before. So he had always covered up with long sleeves and to this day even if he was outside in high temperatures he covered his arms and legs. Of course no-one except his parents knew of this condition and they considered it a direct proclamation from their holy master as payback as they had sinned and fornicated before marriage. They raised him as a freak. And maybe that was why in his defense, he chose the life of an assassin to pay back society and his fellow man.

Bjorn sat alone now after Axel had sauntered out of the shop. The bloke is lazy, Bjorn mumbled disgustedly after him, but I'll go and see what goes on. And he dialed his cousin, Tomas Olafson, who had recently moved to the US and opened a funeral home of all places, in that same town.

Poor Tomas probably needs some consoling he mumbled, after his sister Astrid; my cousin, had been killed in that weird snake biting episode in that God forsaken country.

They were all worldwide assassins.

-35-

The morning passed quickly as Daisy and Reed Conners sat in attorney Billy Miller's office in downtown Minneapolis. It was now after two O'clock as Daisy signed her name to the last page of disclosures and agreements. As they had proceeded, Miller had explained the process that would have to take place before she could be ruled the owner of Roma's estate.

"First off, we need a transfer agreement between countries, Norway and the US. Which I might add, have to go before the civil courts in Norway. A complicated necessity though, and you may have to attend, Miss O'Dell," Miller explained now.

Daisy could only nod. By now her brain was on overload with the complicated process.

"It'll take time for all this Miss O'Dell, but I will keep you abreast," he concluded, standing up at his desk.

Right then, Daisy's stomach growled and she hurriedly stood, hopefully to cover her embarrassment. She had been too nervous to eat anything earlier when they had stopped for lunch.

"Thank you Mr. Miller," she said again extending her hand. "I can be found at my business address during the week and of course at my home, otherwise you can get me on my cell."

"Thank you Miss O'Dell, I'll be getting back to you soon." After Reed had shook hands with the attorney, they left to get back into the elevator and begin the journey down the forty some floors.

Daisy hesitated; she had to get back down, but could she make it down this time without getting sick, or worst yet, fainting? She forced a step into the enclosure and grabbed a hold of the bar on the wall fiercely as the inside of the room began to move. She closed her eyes.

Seeing her distress, Reed put a hand on her shoulder. "Keep your eyes open, Daisy," he said. "We'll be down in a minute."

And finally settling on ground floor after what seemed like hours, Daisy took a deep breath and ran out of the enclosure.

"Daisy, I've got an idea, before we get on the road back to Birch," Reed said catching up with her. "You've got to try to eat something now, so I want to take you to Gina's. The place is a landmark in town." They were in the parking ramp and he opened the car door and waited for her to get settled in the low-slung seat.

"Okay," she said. "I know the place. By now I think I can eat. I was so embarrassed in there when my stomach complained."

"Don't be. We've all had it happen at some time." Reed laughed as he expertly guided the Corvette through the circled driveway down and out of the parking ramp.

Within a few minutes they pulled up to Gina's, Reed's favorite restaurant in Minneapolis. He had known Gina since college when he worked for her in the greasy spoon, as the hamburger café on campus was called.

"I remember this place well," Daisy said, "Both my sons worked here in high school and then in college. They started as dishwashers and then learned to be busboys."

"I didn't know that. I've been coming here for years." Reed put the car in park and soon the two brothers who worked the front came over and opened the car doors.

And after enthusiastic hand shaking and introductions, they remembered Daisy's sons.

Soon Daisy and Reed were whisked in the door to the restaurant where Gina clasped Reed to her ample chest in greeting.

"Good to see you too," he said and smiled at his good friend.

Then her eyes fell on Daisy and she raised a brow at him. "And who is this beautiful lady?"

"This is Daisy O'Dell, a friend and neighbor from Birch." Reed said.

Gina looked her over. "Have you lived there long?" she asked noting Daisy's classy look.

Daisy smiled. "I grew up there and left for twenty years, and moved back a few years ago."

"Really?" Gina laughed, "It must be something in the water."

"Gina," Reed said smiling, "Daisy's sons worked for you. The O'Dell boys." Reed said then.

Gina frowned. "Oh, for God's sake. Do you mean Dylan and Devin, the Delly boys?"

Daisy laughed. "That's them! But I'm sorry Gina, that I never got a chance to meet you those years ago. However, they always spoke well of you."

"Where are those boys now?" Gina asked.

"They both live in Texas. Too far away."

"Greet them from me, will you Daisy. They were two of my best kids." And then Gina led them to a table in the busy dining room. On the way back through the room she stopped a server and instructed him to bring her the check.

Reed and Daisy agreed to relax and have one midday cocktail before they got on the road. Daisy asked, "Reed, do you ever miss a big city?"

"No, not at all," Reed said after taking a drink of his Crown Royal. "Although I just lived here for six years while I attended law school at the U."

Daisy held the straw from her rum collins, and twirled it in her fingers. "I guess I thought it was longer than that. Now I remember, Reed you had your law business in Williston."

"For twenty seven years. Good years," he said nodding his head.

"What prompted you to give it up?" Daisy asked curiously.

She saw pain flash through Reed's eyes and for a minute he was silent. Then he said looking off in the distance, "Earlier my best buddy, Tanner Burke was shot by a nut case back then, and I was there for all those years but it never was the same. Then I decided to make a change. I sold out and moved to Birch and remodeled the old lake place."

"So sorry about losing your best friend, Reed." Daisy looked at him.

"After losing your friend, now you know how I felt. It's a bitch, Daisy. Okay," Reed said then, "let's look at the menus and order some lunch." And they both decided to get the Angus prime rib on fresh crusty pumpernickel bread with the hot au jus. Soon after, Daisy felt better and they were on the road cruising at a steady seventy-five miles an hour.

Three hours later the sun was slowly sliding down in the west as they cruised into Birch Lake. Reed stopped at Daisy's house. As she gathered up her papers and purse, he was already out and opening the car door for her.

"Thank you Reed," Daisy said. "I owe you for all your help."

"Hey, don't mention it. What are neighbors for? But call if you need more help with anything. Or, if you need to go back down to Minneapolis and want company." And he smiled and waved as he got in the Corvette and roared off.

Daisy unlocked her door went in her house. But she stopped in her tracks. Something was wrong!

-36-

The minute Daisy stepped into her house back in Birch Lake she knew something was amiss. She stood still for a minute as her senses sorted out the reason her intuition went to instant alert.

Ordinarily, she liked her things in precise perfect spots around her house, and to her eye, it wasn't that anything was messed up or particularly out of order. But that some things just seemed slightly off. The basket of folded napkins that stood on the cupboard wasn't messy, but stood just a fraction too far in the middle of the counter top. And the large fluffy scatter rug that lay under the dining table and chairs in the breakfast area hadn't been moved but the long pile on it had shifted as if it had been lifted here and there to search under it.

Somehow she felt that whoever had been in her house had left now, but she still hesitatingly took a few steps further into the room and searched the floor and corners as she proceeded. Well now, not only was she spooked about there still might be more snakes in her house, now she had the added anxiety of knowing someone had been able to come and go in her space.

On faltering steps she walked through the living room, the sun room and then her bedroom. Here her intuition jumped into high gear as she stood another minute. Then something told her to go to her walk-in closet, and check her dresser drawers, see if anything there had been moved.

Oh for God's sake, she yelled to the walls as she stood in the cedar-lined room and pulled out the drawers. Now she knew someone had been there too! Instead of her underwear being folded in her own particular way now the colors and the seamed edges were just slightly reversed. In her drawer of bras here too, she could see they had been disturbed. She slammed the drawers shut and hurried out of the room.

Now who the hell was doing this and for what reason? Should she call Reed back or Sheriff Montes? Or Ed? She hadn't talked to Ed for several days now, before she had gone to Minneapolis. And for God's sake, now she had Romeo, that pesky dog to worry about, she remembered as she hurried back through her lovely rooms.

Well, first of all she had to get him from the kennels, and then she'd turn him loose in the house to do his sleuthing while she went down to her shop and checked that place out. God only knows what that might look like.

Romeo, the little shit was glad to see her when she scooped him out of the pen he'd been kept in. Licking her face as she bent to hook the leash on his collar, she wrinkled her nose at his doggy breath.

Yes, yes I'm glad to see you too, she mumbled to his excited greeting. Then back at her house she opened the door and shooed him into the kitchen. Now check it out and I'll be back shortly, she commanded the little pile of rags as he took off running with his nose to the floor.

It was now dark as Daisy drove through the quiet streets of Birch, and the only cars around were nosed up close to the Legion Bar. As she passed by the building she could hear the resounding beat of a bass guitar from the juke box as it played to its dedicated masses. Then in the next block she unlocked the door to her nail shop and flipped on the lights. Cautious now, she stood in the door and let her eyes roam her two rooms. The familiar and tangy smell of acrylics and acetone bit her nostrils as usual, but nothing else. Then stepping in, after a few minutes she could see nothing had been disturbed. Locking up, Daisy sucked in her breath at that relief.

Driving back home, she had a fleeting thought; maybe it's all just my imagination. After all, my nerves are fried after the meeting with Billy Miller, the attorney. By now she was totally bushed after the long day on the road to and from Minneapolis, and then while there, her anxieties about starting to claim her inheritance from Roma's estate. Maybe she shouldn't have gone forward with it and just put the note away for a good memory. She punched the leather covered steering wheel while driving through the quiet streets of Birch at the sudden down-turn of her intended quiet life.

After driving in the garage and going into her house through the garage door, she quietly opened the door into the kitchen and stood for a minute. Instantly she heard Romeo's toenails clacking on the wood floors as he scampered to greet her. Then he nudged her over to his spot on the kitchen floor that he had claimed as his gifting area. When she followed him over her eyes bugged when she saw what he had gathered for her. Not only was there an assortment of spiders and a small mouse, as she bent down to see better, there was a rolled up piece of paper. It reminded Daisy of what they'd called a spitball when she'd been a kid. She picked it up. It felt damp, probably from Romeo's mouth as he had carried it over she thought. She unrolled it carefully and was just barely able to discern what was written. The message read, "O'Dell knows too much, she has to die." And her address was there. Daisy froze as she stood looking at it. Then she walked on shaking legs over to the counter and sat. She stared again at it and swallowed over a lump of fear in her throat.

What did it mean? She knew too much about what? Shivers swept over her as she realized this must have fallen out of the intruders pocket as he had pilfered through her personal belongings.

Romeo stood silently at her side and then snuffled her ankles like he was waiting for praise. Daisy bent down and rubbed his head and said, "Good boy", then he contentedly ran off again on another search.

Daisy had to call Reed. When he picked up and listened to her breathless explanation of these new developments, he told her to immediately get out of the house and to report this evident break-in to Jesse, Birch Lake's sheriff. She had just moved back into her home after the big hullabaloo with the snakes.

"Get back to me as soon as you relocate," Reed advised now on the phone. Daisy hung up and took a breath.

For God's sake, she yelled to the walls. Where the hell am I supposed to go? Back to the motel? As she sat at the counter now, the phone rang. When she answered, Ed was on the other end.

"Hey stranger," he said, "I've missed you the last days. Are you okay?"

"Not really," Daisy finally confessed.

"Why, what's wrong?" Ed insisted.

"I need to get out of my house again. Something's happened!" Daisy said and her breath hitched in her throat.

'What?" Ed asked. "Tell me!"

"It's a long story Ed. Can you meet me at the restaurant?" Daisy asked, "I can be there in five minutes."

"Give me ten; I just need to close the sales office." And Ed turned down the lights in the new and used car lots.

Daisy grabbed a jacket and her purse and went out in the darkened garage and slid in her car. When she fired up the Porsche and put it into reverse to back out, the sound of the clicking door locks reassured her of safety.

At the restaurant, the dinner crowd had left and Flo had cleaned up the dining room and was sitting at a table near the kitchen enjoying a peaceful cup of coffee and a cigarette. This was her night to work until closing at ten, and she had an hour left.

"Hello, Flo," Daisy said. "Okay if I take a booth and have some iced tea?" She asked.

"Of course my dear, I'll bring it right over." Flo said brightly, but as she stood up her back barked a sharp retort over her moving again. She would have to take the hot-water bottle to bed again tonight, she guessed. Ed Harrison came in then and joined Daisy in the booth. My, my, Flo thought to herself, is there something going on between those two, she wondered? And she scooped up two waters to bring over.

"Thanks Ed for meeting me," Daisy said then. "I'm sorry I haven't had time to see you these last days. So much has gone on. I was down in the Minneapolis today to see an attorney."

"Why," Ed asked. "Are you okay?"

"I'm not so sure Ed. You won't believe what has happened!" And Daisy told him about finding the letter in Roma's make-up bag giving all her finances and possessions to her.

Ed shook his head at her tirade of events. "I don't know what to say Daisy. What happened tonight when you got home then, from Minneapolis?"

Daisy's face was pale and her lips were stiff. She had put the soggy note Romeo had found in a clear plastic baggie before leaving the house. She took it out of her purse now and began telling him of what she'd found at her house when she got home earlier.

"Jesus H Christ, Daisy," he swore, "First, I'm taking you over to see Jesse to make an official report and then you've got to come back to my house to stay. It's not safe for you to be alone."

By now, all her fight was gone and Daisy was so tired, she could only agree.

-37-

Bjorn Olafson sat in the business office/living room of his Cousin Tomas Olafson's home in Birch Lake and slurped nosily on his dark roast coffee. It was a big one story home with the basement outfitted with the necessary equipment needed for the mortuary business. When Bjorn looked around the office/living room, he guessed it could be a comfortable place to sit and read a book and relax on the plaid couches, but Tomas had also said it was where a grieving family sat and discussed the details of getting their dead ready for burial. And he had said right through those double doors downstairs was where the gruesome duties of his profession took place. Bjorn just shook his head at his cousin's shocking doings and wondered whatever had made Olaf take up such a ghastly front.

Cousin Tomas, the town's undertaker who helped doc, had been busy the last few weeks shipping bodies over the ocean back home to Norway. First, he had to send his Cousin Astrid's body back to be received by the family for the huge memorial service they had planned. Then inside of a week or so, he'd had to patch up the back of Gunther's head, another cousin and get his remains ready to send over the ocean. After all the angry hand wringing, the outraged Olafson and Mueller families had agreed, that someone had to go back over to the US, that world of crazies, and seek revenge for stealing two of their own people. Two of its valuable members, who contributed hugely to the family coffers. And Bjorn, youngest son of the families was next up, they had decided. So he had packed a bag and undertook the mission.

All he knew so far was that a woman named O'Dell had to die. And he was to take care of her termination. He'd been informed by the family elders 'that was all he needed to know.' And they had informed him that he should search O'Dell's home for the cash, because someone had cleaned out Gunther's pockets as he was known to carry huge amounts on his person in a money belt.

"For Christ's sake, I was ready to take care of that bitch but she wasn't there," Bjorn growled. "Fuck, I wasted all day but I had time to look through that "huset", I couldn't find any god dammed "penga," he bellyached.

Bjorn Olafson played with his van dyke beard as he studied his Americanized cousin Tomas. Bjorn had been instructed to contact Tomas to let him know he was there in the US, in case things went awry and Tomas's undertaking services were needed again, his family had advised. There was no love lost and never had been between the two cousins, as when as kids Bjorn had been teased unmercilessly by his cousins because he was hairy. They'd taunted and called him Cousin It, like a character in the old US Adams Family TV series. Once as nine year olds, they'd held him down and torn off his clothes and pulled at the hair on his body.

Bjorn swallowed his revulsion now as he remembered his shame, so painful at that tender age. But over the years he's toughened up his feelings and now he didn't give a fuck. The only person he had feelings for in this world was a sister who had run away from the families when she was sixteen and joined a convent. Bjorn was the only one she had contacted years later, only to wring the promise out of him that he wouldn't tell a soul of her whereabouts. Over the years Bjorn had supported the nunnery with generous donations of his ill gotten currency. And the humble convent took his money without asking questions.

"Too bad Astrid croaked," Tomas Olafson mumbled now about his sister as they drank their coffee.

"Yah, yah," Bjorn answered. "Too bad, snakes they say. What the fuck is that about?"

"Astrid, my esteemed sister, was supposed to take out Roma Hurst, but those reptiles or whatever got her instead." Olaf refilled their coffee and then blew loudly on the hot liquid.

"Serves her right," Bjorn commented dryly. Remembering her childhood jeers he went on, "thinking she had the smarts. Maybe she'd still be alive if she'd stayed out of our business."

Tomas took a loud slurp of his coffee. This cousin looked a lot different from Bjorn, where as Bjorn was blond, Tomas was a redhead. Red hair, red beard and red blustery colored skin. Both men were born in Oslo to brothers. The Olafson and Mueller families made millions in the ship building enterprises known worldwide. By the time this generation came along there wasn't much work that had to be done except to collect their revenues. And to these spoiled siblings there wasn't much they hadn't tried and when they found out they liked to kill, this was when they hired themselves out. Of course, this was a well-kept secret, known only to the ship-building fathers, and the cohort cousins. Tomas, Bjorn and Astrid Olafson, and Gunther Mueller, the other cousin.

"Well, there's just the two of us left. You know what this means, don't you?" Bjorn mumbled to Tomas the undertaker.

"Yah, it means we'll have the lot of it," Tomas said. "Himil, I'll be busy with all these "merkins" here. But I'm seeing that they don't hire too much. They buy their own guns to do their deeds."

"Well, then take a holiday." Bjorn suggested. Actually he didn't give a damn about Tomas and had been glad when the bugger moved to the states, but until the old folks croaked, he had to keep his peace so his inheritance would not be fucked up. After that when he got his take from the family business, he'd give them the finger and move far away. He'd start over in the "for hire" business by himself.

It was getting late and Bjorn was tired of talking to his stupid cousin.

"Where do you go in this town?" He asked now.

"There's only one place. It's called the Legion." Tomas remarked.

"What is it?" Bjorn asked. He was a social snob and only subjected himself to the pomp and circumstance of Norwegian culture.

"Well," Olaf snickered to himself, "It's a quaint place, so you'd have to see it." He had a hard time keeping an innocent look on his face.

"Well then, I'll go," Bjorn stood up, glad to get out and away from this man's cloying malodorous house.

He got in his Range Rover and found the only place in town that had a smattering of vehicles parked next to the door. Music with the beat much like jungle drums echoed and clouds of cigarette smoke blew out on the streets from an exhaust fan.

Bjorn Olafson crowded the Range Rover in next to a dusty bent up pick-up loaded with feed sacks and when he opened the wide door of his vehicle it smacked right into the side of this old yellow eye sore.

Fucking "merkins" he growled, "Get out of my way!"

-38-

Daisy hurried home to pack after meeting Ed Harrison at the Woodsmen café, and after his invitation to stay at his house for awhile. "Just until things quieted down," she'd said. Now she looked around her lovely home and felt heartsick at how things were going. She'd always loved her house and had been right beside her builder when it was being built. She had designed the layout and had spent hours with an architect putting those ideas into a blueprint. That was almost ten years ago now and even yet, she loved coming home to her place. But now after the last few weeks, she was appalled at her feelings of dread at opening the door.

She still shuddered at the thought of those snakes slithering around in her things. And, also finding that stranger, dead in her kitchen after being bitten by one of those poisonous snakes. It seemed like years since she had been getting ready for Roma's visit and now look at all the unbelievable things that had happened. And that she was being driven out of her home again because of all that horror.

Damn, she was tired of it, so tired of one thing after another going on. But now she hurried into her bedroom and got out a big suitcase and laid it on her bed and began to throw underwear, jeans and shirts and then make-up into it, and hurriedly carried it to the kitchen door and clunked it down.

"Romeo," she called then and the busy little pile of rags came scuttling into the kitchen. This time he hadn't had time to bring a present but a doughnut hole size pile of lint sat on top of his nose. When he saw Daisy held the door open into that same old torture chamber that she called a carrier, he put his brakes on and skidded to a quick stop on the wooden floor.

No way was he getting in that cramped jailhouse! For God's sake, last time he'd had to hold going pee for hours on that long ride home from that crazy house she called a kennel. Didn't she know it was a dishonorable place filled with lawbreakers and misfits? Gang fights were common, and that last time he'd had to hide behind the water cooler or else that big black rogue with those ridiculous small brown ears who stood as tall as a grownup, would have eaten him alive. No way! But then, he had to change his mind as she just rolled him up in a ball and stuffed him in there anyway.

"There you go, you little shit. Now if you're good, you can come along with me over to Ed's house. But you'd better be good or else you're going back to the kennel." At that awful threat, Romeo smiled showing his teeth at her, to let her know he would be on his best behavior.

Ed Harrison lived on the edge of town, right down on the Birch Lake's shore. Like Reed Conners, he too had cleared and sanded an area and made a perfect beach. Here he had beach chairs and an umbrella topped table, and numerous chaise loungers set out in the park like scene. Daisy parked the Porsche and let Romeo out of his carrier. Then she grabbed the suitcase and walked to the door.

She rang the bell on the carved wood double door and just then Ed opened it wearing an apron over his jeans and t-shirt.

"Welcome, as chili is the only thing I know how to cook, its simmering now and I've got a bottle of red ready. Come on in." Ed exclaimed throwing open the door. Romeo stood politely on the porch waiting for his invitation but the grownups just about closed the door on him. Finally, Ed saw him and whistled for him to come in.

"First of all, let's get you settled, Daisy." Ed exclaimed and picked up her suitcase and led the way to a guestroom on the other side of the house from where she stayed before.

"By the way, I've got that side of the house closed off and am having it redone," he explained nodding toward the north side of the big house.

"Thanks Ed. For a minute I thought about not coming back here where I had killed that maniac. But I'm okay."

"Good, but if your uncomfortable being here Daisy, we can go to the hotel at the casino and stay." She noticed that he said, 'we'.

"Well, we'll see," she murmured. The room he took her to was done beautifully in greens and cream and had a huge bed covered in a fluffy down cover. Plump pillows leaned against a padded forest green leather headboard and a mink throw lay at the foot of the bed for cold toes. Silk covered lampshades topped crystal lamps and the soft light glowed throughout the room.

"This is lovely Ed," Daisy exclaimed as she stood on a Persian rug.

"Thanks. The bath is right through that door," Ed said as he set her case on a stand. "If you want to rest a minute, go ahead while I set a table and open the wine to breathe." He shut the door behind himself and left her to look around. She sat down in one of the matching slipper chairs in front of a bow window and put her head back on the top. She was dead tired and could have slid between the covers easily, but manners prevailed and she had to meet up with Ed in the kitchen and attempt to enjoy his chili and wine.

As she sat now, with her aching head resting on top of the chair, a sob erupted in her throat and escaped her lips. She straightened up quickly. For God's sake, she couldn't lose it now. She needed to keep herself together and get through this whole dilemma and keep her business open, and, she had to get over hating to go home. Now she had this added worry of this bizarre offer of Roma's to keep her up nights.

It was almost too much for her to deal with. She'd always been a responsible person with a decent appreciation of her own rights, but now she felt she had been wrung inside out by the emotional needs of other people. Unintentionally of course, she had to add.

Just then, Ed knocked on the bedroom door.

"Daisy," he said meaning well, "come on out and eat."

"Thanks, I'll be right there," Daisy exclaimed.

She sat up and shook her head to wake up. She stepped into the bathroom for a quick once over with her hair-brush and lip-gloss, while thinking, now what about Ed? Would he accept just friendship? Well, she'd have to play this one by ear and just see how things went.

She hurried through the rooms and to the kitchen where she found him. "Follow me, Daisy I set us up in the dining room." he said and led her into the room.

"My goodness Ed," she exclaimed, "You shouldn't have gone to all this."

"Well, why not?" He laughed, holding a chair for her. She took the seat and looked around at the table.

Set for two, the black linen topped table was aglow from the huge silver candelabra, crystal glassware and silver plate chargers and matching black fan shaped napkins sitting atop paper thin china plates. A bottle of red wine sat nestled in a silver ice bucket.

"It's lovely," Daisy said spreading a napkin in her lap. Ed sat and picked up her soup plate and filled it with chili, then handed her a basket of hot popovers.

"My goodness," she exclaimed again then, "how come some smart woman hasn't snapped you up ages ago to warm her bed?"

Ed said easily. "No one has offered lately."

Hmm- sensing this conversation could get dicey, Daisy tasted the chili and took a drink of the wine. And touching her lips with the napkin, she quickly changed the subject.

"Yumm- this is delicious," she murmured. And they were both quiet then and began to eat as the strains of classical music emanated from the in-house speakers.

Sitting back after eating, Ed picked up the wine bottle and glasses. "Come on, let's sit in the living room by the fire and finish this." He said then waiting for her to follow.

Daisy was dead tired, especially after such a sumptuous meal but not wanting to be impolite, she did. They both sat down on a couch and he refilled their glasses.

Then a strange thing happened. The lights flickered on and off several times, and then the room was left in pitch black darkness. The music stopped. Then to Daisy's horror, she felt Ed struggle for a few seconds and then felt his weight lift up off the couch. All was still for a second and she sat frozen. Then suddenly as hands closed around her throat, her blood-curdling scream stopped midway as it bounced off the walls in Ed Harrison's living room in Birch Lake.

-39-

The room had gone black, and in the darkness Daisy felt Ed leave the couch, heard him groan and then heard a thud on the floor. Seconds later, she felt cold hands close around her throat from behind and in that moment had the terrible frightening thought that she was going to die. Now! But instinctively she remembered a quick death defying hold she had learned in a self-defense class and she jerked her body forward pulling her attacker off his stance, and in that split second brought her elbows up and with all her strength aimed them backwards into his solar plexus. And suddenly as the assailant struggled for air he loosened his hold and she broke free. Springing off the couch and flying out of the house, she ran for the

Porsche and using the handy fingertip entrance jumped in and sped away. A few blocks over at the sheriff's office, she was relieved to find Jesse still at his desk busy with a pile of papers.

Running in she yelled, "Jesse, something's happened to Ed!"

Jesse stood up hurriedly and his chair fell backwards in his haste. "Where?" Was all he had time to say.

"Over at his place." Daisy leaned in and braced her hands on his desk and tried to ease her gasping breath.

"What happened?" Jesse asked as he grabbed a jacket and adjusted his holstered gun.

"We were sitting on the couch when the lights went out. I couldn't see who it was. Oh God," Daisy wailed, "Someone tried to choke me, but I got away. Jesse it's them again!"

"Who?" Jesse roared.

"The same ones who have been doing all this." Daisy sank down in a chair and put her head in her hands.

"Okay, stay here with my deputy and I'll go check it out." Jesse ran out and the LTD spewed gravel as he sped out into the street and disappeared.

Daisy found a Kleenex in her pocket and blew her nose. For God's sake, now they'd hurt Ed. What if they had killed him too? He was just a nice guy helping her. Oh God, oh God, she wailed.

What could she go?   She would be next!   She couldn't go back to her house or the motel again? They'd easily find her.

There was no safe place except in her car and abruptly without a word to the deputy she ran out to her Porsche again and began to drive.

Three hours later and nearing midnight she hit the heavy traffic of downtown Minneapolis. Then nearing the underground parking for the Grand Hotel she hurriedly locked up. Thank goodness, she hadn't had time to bring her suitcase in at Ed's house, so she had clothes to wear.

The hotel was an up-scale place and at the desk she asked to see Mr. Bleeker, the owner. The place was a land-mark around town and she had worked there for years in her marriage when her family was young. Their bills had been huge even though her husband camped out nights and week-ends in their basement working with his computers and mountains of books. It had been years before he hit it big in his medical field.

Mr. Bleeker came out of the back offices and broke into a smile when he recognized Daisy.

"My dear girl, how nice to see you," he said and crushed her to his chest in a bear hug.

"John, it's good to see you too."   She stepped back and caught her breath, then returned his smile.

"Are you in town for long?" he asked.

"A few days," then she asked, "John, I need to ask you a favor."

"Anything, do you need money, a job, a husband, just name it?" He laughed, then saw she didn't join in. "Okay, sorry," he added, "it's serious then?"

"John," she whispered, "I need help. I don't have any money or ID along and I need to hide out. I don't want anyone to know I'm here."

"Okay," he said without asking questions. "Let me get a key and get you settled." And he disappeared behind the desk for a minute, then came back and took her suitcase. "We'll take my private elevator up," he said then.

At the tenth floor, they stepped out, and here there were only several rooms located discreetly away from each other. Of course, Daisy was familiar with them as working room service those years ago she had delivered orders numerous times to special guests.

"Daisy, you will not be listed anywhere as a guest and when you order room service ask for Olaf. He will take care of you. Now call me if you need anything, and don't hesitate for a minute."

They were standing right inside the door in the foyer and then he went ahead to the bedroom with her suitcase and set it on the stand.

"Have you had anything to eat, should I send Olaf up now with a snack?" Mr. Bleeker asked coming back to stand by her in the sitting room.

Daisy's knees almost gave out from exhaustion. This was the second time she had come to Minneapolis that day. The same day for God's sake. And now, knowing she would be safe at least for awhile, she had to lie down quickly or else she felt she would just melt away into the carpet from fatigue. But she managed to say, "John, thank you, but I'll be fine."

"Okay, now put the locks on the door and get to sleep, my dear." And he quickly went out.

Taking her cell phone out of her pocket the first thing she did after the door closed was call the sheriff department back in Birch Lake. But there was no answer, and even though it was late at night a deputy should have been there on night duty. Did she know Jesse's cell number? She realized she didn't have her phone book of course. She tried Ed's house but of course there wasn't any answer there either. Finally after pacing the floor Daisy fell into the lovely down filled feather bed.

When she awoke the next day, at first, she was puzzled at the unfamiliar surroundings and the sounds coming from outside. Even though she was ten stories up the hum of traffic and car horns still echoed through the walls. Then as she laid in the warm cocoon of the fluffy comforter the scary details of the day before came screeching back into her thoughts.

What had happened to Ed? Dear God, was he okay?

She grabbed her cell phone and called his home number again this morning, but after it rang ten times and there was still no answer. Her heart hammered in her chest. Next she called Jesse at his office even though it was just going on seven am.

When his deputy answered she asked for the sheriff.

"Jesse, this is Daisy. Did you find Ed last night?" She whispered when he picked up.

"Yep, I found him on the living room floor out cold. He's in ER now for tests but it looks like he's going to be okay. Where are you? My deputy said you ran out of here last night."

"I'm in Minneapolis Jesse, I just kept driving."

"I found a black glove on the kitchen floor under a chair. But I couldn't find a mate for it in Ed's coat closet so it must belong to the assailant. And oh yeah, my deputy dropped your dog off at the kennel this morning."

"Oh for God's sake, I forgot about the little shit! Thanks. Jesse, it was that same mad-man who killed Roma who did this! He was after me!"

"Well, we'll get him Daisy. Now, you just stay put there for awhile."

She called the hospital next and found Ed Harrison listed and got connected to his room.

"Ed," she said hoarsely when he answered, "Thank God!" Was all she could say at the moment at the sound of his voice.

"Daisy, are you okay?" "He asked anxiously.

"Ed, he tried to choke me but I got away and I'm fine now." She sank down on the bed in her room at the Grand Hotel in Minneapolis and massaged her neck.

"Christ, the asshole almost paralyzed me for good, but I'm okay."

"You've got to hide Ed," Daisy whispered. "He'll know where to find you."

"Don't worry Daisy I've got a guard at my door so I'm safe for now."

"Thank God," Daisy said and hurriedly hung up after saying, "Ed, I'll stay in touch." But it would be weeks before she did.

-40-

Jesse looked up from his paperwork as Reed Conners strolled into his office and took a chair by his desk.

"Morning," Jesse said to his friend. "What's up? Your message said you had an idea you wanted to run by me."

"Yeah, you know, after I heard what happened last night to Daisy and Ed almost getting killed by that same asshole, I couldn't get to sleep." Reed leaned back in the chair and shook his head.

"I hope it's better than the ideas I've been coming up with since then." Jesse reached for a cigar and put the unlit stogy between his lips.

"Jesse, we know that someone took over after we got Mueller and is still lurking around here somewhere. And he knows that Daisy is not in her house and is hiding out somewhere else."

"Yeah." Jesse fingered the lighter in his shirt pocket as he listened.

"So," Reed went on, "the fucker will probably be quiet for awhile now. Probably stay hidden for a few days thinking he's giving her false hopes that he has up and left. And he'll just wait and watch for her to come back to her house."

"Okay," Jesse nodded listening.

"So, let's wait a few days and then I'll go over and stay in there, quietly, of course. In the evenings I'll turn on a few lights, and I'll be ready!"

"Maybe--, but if he's watching, how the hell are we going to get you in her house?" Jesse asked.

"Hm—but don't worry, I haven't figured that out yet." Reed stood up. "Have you had breakfast yet?"

"No," Jesse grumbled. "The wife is gone again."

"Come on, I'm buying," Reed offered and Jesse locked up as his deputy was not in as yet, and they walked the block over to the Woodsmen café. The late summer morning breeze carried the luscious aroma of bacon and cinnamon rolls as they neared the café and as they stepped in, Flo greeted them with her usual smile.

"Hello boys," she said, as she was known to do to almost all her male customers in town, as she was old enough to be anyone's grandma for miles around, she claimed. Except Otto of course, who was one year older, she would oft times clarify. She carried two ice waters, cups and a steaming pot of coffee on her tray and hurried over in her crepe soled nurse's shoes and busily set things down on their table-top.

"I just took a pan of cinnamon rolls out of the oven. Should I bring you some?" She asked, and then stood with pencil poised over her order pad ready to write.

"Absolutely. And eggs, bacon and some cakes. Is that good for you Jesse?"

"Sounds like manna from heaven. I had cold beans and chips for supper last night."

"Is your wife out gallivanting again Jesse?" Flo asked.

"Yeah, yeah, seems she's gone a lot lately," Jesse grumbled. "Way it looks, I'll probably be spending a lot of my retirement home alone." He finally lit his cigar and blew smoke upwards to the exhaust fan. "Well, that would be okay too," he added.

Reed smiled at his friend, and was too nice to add anything negative about the man's wife. But it was well known that Mrs. Ortega didn't treat Jesse very well.

"Daisy called me last night," Jesse said now. "She's in Minneapolis and intends to stay there, but I will call her and get her permission to use her house to draw this one out."

"Okay," Reed said, and then looking confused remarked, "She's in the cities? We were just there yesterday. She went back?"

"Yeah, said she was so scared after the second killer tried to choke her over at Ed's house, she just got in her car and drove."

"Goddamn." Reed took a long drink of his coffee after adding cream and sugar. He asked, "Have you heard how Ed is doing over at the hospital?"

"I talked to the guard at his door over there and he said the doctor is going to release him this afternoon."

Reed shook his head, "You know, we better warn him to be on his guard, both at his car lot, and at home."

"You're right, and I better do it now." Jesse took his cell out of his shirt pocket and called the hospital and got the guard on the line and passed on that information. And just then Flo came out of the kitchen with a loaded tray and expertly set it on a stand.

"Now boys, you can't leave until you have cleaned your plates. I gave you some home fries to go with your eggs."

"Oh boy, I can feel the cholesterol already clogging my arteries," Reed commented looking at all the food, but smiled and added, "but I'll force myself to eat this."

After breakfast the two men parted with Jesse saying, "I'll check with Daisy and get her permission to use her house and get back to you."

Two nights later, Reed put on dark clothes, packed artillery in a bag with a change of clothes, and caught a ride into town to meet Jesse at his office.

After working out the details of their surveillance, Reed waited at his office till after ten and then quietly slipped out the back door and was soon in Daisy's neighborhood. Carrying his bag he dodged the houses that were lit up and quietly slipped through the darkened streets and alleys. At Daisy's house, on the porch in the back he found the pot of flowers that covered the key and was inside in a few seconds, the .38 in his hand. He dropped the bag by the door.

The house was in total darkness except for a very dim nightlight in the kitchen where he stood so he could see his way around in there, but the rest of the place was dark. He stood for a few minutes in the gloomy darkness and let his eyes adjust. He had been to Daisy's house several times over the years and vaguely remembered the floor plan. And now first of all, he needed to check it out first to be sure the new killer wasn't in there already waiting for her to come home.

Taking a small flashlight out of his pocket he crept quietly through the house looking in closets and under beds and behind furniture. He even looked in a pantry and under a low shelf that held large appliances. He finally convinced himself, that the place was clear. He also thought that if the asshole was watching the house, he would think it was Daisy herself checking for any intrusion.

Think again fucker, Reed grumbled to the silence. Taking a thermos out of his bag, he poured a cup of caffeine loaded coffee and sat down to wait in the living room. He had opened a drape a few inches to let in a shaft of moonlight so the room was illuminated just a bit, enough for him to see anything that moved and with a clear view into her bedroom where he had also turned on a nightlight. Also using an old trick he had used before, he rolled up pillows to make it look like Daisy was sleeping in her bed.

Then he sat in an easy chair and sipped his coffee, his guns were laid out within easy reach. He had also done some research on stun guns when he had been in Minneapolis on his last case and had gotten several for himself realizing it was something he should have in his business and he had one handy in his shirt pocket, and in the other his cell phone. He and Jesse had worked out a system where as soon as he recognized signs that the killer was close or had shown up, Reed would immediately punch the speed dial and Jesse could be there in three minutes. They also figured Reed would be able to stay there now through the night, the next day and until midnight and then he had to get out. And if the asshole hadn't shown up by then, after an eight hour respite they'd do it again.

Now Reed began the wait. One thing he had learned in his investigative career was how to stay awake and alert. He had never told anyone, that one thing that worked for him was he always carried a "rubrics cube" along in his bag. And even in the semi darkness of the house tonight he would spend hours working out new strategies on how to solve the puzzle. This had kept him alert, time and again, when he felt himself began to drift in times past, and, he could spend hours at it and still listen and watch for any intrusiveness that might occur.

Now it was going on three o'clock in the morning and he had solved the rubric cube's mystery twice. He put the plastic object down and reached for his thermos for some coffee. As he was turning the cork in the top of the container, he heard something. He wasn't sure what or where it had come from, but he put the thermos down carefully on the floor, and grabbed the .38, relieved, he hadn't pulled the cork out of the thermos and released the aroma of coffee in the house.

Reed didn't move but sat still and listened. Everything was still, with not another sound. Maybe it had been the house shifting in the night, he thought as a few minutes went by without another sound. He reached in his shirt pocket for his stun gun and held that in his left hand ready. When he thought about it, maybe it hadn't even been an audible sound, but an inaudible one of movement, made by someone right outside the house. Yes, there it was again, he realized and listened and then speed dialed Jesse as arranged. He got up out of the chair and slipped to the hallway right outside the doorway to Daisy's bedroom. He pressed close to the frame and listened, but there was nothing. He didn't move, he hardly dared take a breath. With his eyes glued on the glass patio doors across the room that led out to the pool from her bedroom, this was surely where he would come in Reed surmised, and they had purposely left the door unlocked. Then all of a sudden, he saw stars and felt the side of his head explode with pain as he was hit. His knees buckled and he began to feel himself go down.

"Goddamn the fucker got me --," he heard a whisper and realized it must have been himself murmuring faintly. Everything began to turn black as he slid to the floor, and then gun shots rang out in the bedroom of Daisy's house.

-41-

Instantly awake after getting Reed's call, Jesse Ortega rolled off the couch in his office where he'd slept the last few nights to be closer to Daisy's house when he got the call from Reed. On the way out the door he holstered his guns and grabbed his hat, then climbed in his car. He'd taken his wife's new one back to the office tonight as it was quieter to run and easier to maneuver since it was the latest, smallest Ford model.

Daisy's house was three blocks over and he was there in just under the three minutes they had worked out. He jumped out of the Ford and ran like hell to her backyard, staying close against the wall. He ran over to the unlocked patio door and opened it, just as they had arranged earlier too.

And just inside as Reed was hit, the killer knocked the .38 out of his right hand and it had gone skittering across the floor. And as Reed's head hit the floor, the fall was just enough to jar him out of the fog, and he took aim with his left hand with the stun gun which he had clung to. The killer stood just a foot away with his back turned pointing a gun at Daisy's bed when Reed summoned the last vestige of strength and got to his knees and reached out and jammed the stun gun into the killer's back. The intruder had gotten off two quick shots at the rolled up pillows in Daisy's bed, when in that same instant, Jesse charged into the room with his revolver aimed right at the man's head. At the explosion of Jesse's gun, the killer went down, spilling his blood and brains all over Daisy's beautifully decorated room covering the bed linens, walls and carpets with gore.

"Are you okay?" Jesse yelled to Reed as he had frantically looked around and found a light switch on a wall, then stared at the mess around him in the glare.

Reed struggled to his feet and growled when he saw some of blood had settled on his jacket and jeans, and then even felt some on his face.

"Goddamn it," he said and went into Daisy's bathroom and grabbed a towel to wipe his face and came back out where Jesse stood with his gun still out and ready. Jesse bent down then and felt for a pulse on the body even though death was evident and when he didn't find one, he holstered his gun.

"The asshole is dead," he said. "I'll call Doc to come over and pick him up."

Reed came back to stand by his side after locating his .38 in a corner of the room.

"That was close," he said to Jesse. "He came out of nowhere and got me and my .38 went flying. Goddamn." He swiped at his hair and added, "As I hit the floor, thank God, I still had the stun gun in my hand."

"You were lucky, my friend. Man, it's a good thing I deputized you earlier. Now, finally my town can have some peace." Jesse took off his sheriff's cap and put an arm up and wiped his face off on his shirt sleeve. "And, we can get some sleep, for Christ's sake."

The whole incident had only taken about four minutes and it was going on three thirty in the morning. The night had gotten cloudy and dark without a moon.

"Come on, let's get out of here," Reed nodded for Jesse to follow and they went to find the lights in the kitchen to wait for Doc, who was the coroner, and the medical examiner for Birch Lake.

"I'll wait until morning to call Daisy, but I'll have to call the BCA tonight to come over from Bemidji to start their investigation." Jesse went on, "Oh yeah, it's going to be a hell of a circus again before we can really have some peace here."

"Well, look at it this way, Birch Lake is on the map now and a place where you can find some action." Reed commented trying for a lighter moment.

"Yeah, it's that. Come on outside, I need a cigar." And they stepped out the kitchen door onto a deck that held a table and pillow covered chairs and loungers.

"And I'll join you." Reed noticed his own hand shook slightly as he took the pack of cigarettes and a lighter out of the inside pocket of his jacket. He lit up and took a deep drag of his Marlboro. "Goddamn, I don't know when this tasted so good," he grumbled.

As they were finishing their smokes headlights flared across the front lawn as Doc's van hurdled into the driveway. They hurried to the front of the house and greeted him as he pulled a gurney out of the back of his vehicle and popped the wheels.

"God awful time to do this," he grumbled, nodding a greeting at Reed and Jesse. "Where is the body?"

"Follow me," Jesse said and they walked to the front. Jesse asked Reed, "could you go in the house and unlock the front door please? It'll be easier for Doc to get in and out through there."

It took another couple of hours for the Doc to slip into his medical examiner mode and take notes and pictures before they loaded the body onto the gurney. He had also taken fingerprints and DNA samples as they had no idea who the body belonged to.

"Okay guys, I'm done here and the body will be at my funeral home for the BCA. I'll send in the prints to see if we'll get an ID. And I suppose the big guys will be back if we find out he was another international killer," Doc proclaimed as he opened the door to his van and got in and spun off into the night.

"Let's get out of here and get some sleep," Jesse said and they walked back into Daisy's house and locked up. They both realized neither one had wheels nearby and took off on foot to the Ford Jesse had driven. When they got to Reed's place, he got out and waved a tired hand and Jesse spun off. When Reed got inside his house, the luscious aroma of coffee greeted him and he hurried to his kitchen as Lindy Lewis' familiar voice called out, "Good morning sweetheart!"

-42-

Daisy had spent the last few days having a lovely time sleeping late and eating sumptuous meals at some of the new upscale restaurants around Minneapolis, as she waited to hear from Jesse back home in Birch Lake to give her the all clear sign that it was safe to come back. She had time now to also look up old friends and even a lover she'd taken up with years ago while she was in the throes of the long drawn out divorce from the great Vaughn O'Dell. Sadly, that re-acquaintance proved a mistake as now the man she had thought so suave and savvy turned out to be just another phony player.

Thank God, she murmured now as she sipped her morning coffee from room service, she hadn't fallen for his scheming ways when she'd been so vulnerable. Just then her cell phone rang and when she answered, Jesse's booming voice greeted her.

"Daisy," he said. "We got the perpetrator last night, so you can come home soon now."

"Oh Lord, that's good to hear Jesse, but is everyone okay?" She asked.

"Oh yeah, we're fine. Reed was there." He added.

"Who was this person?" Daisy's voice shook now.

"A man, we don't know who yet. But we sent his DNA off so we should know soon."

"Okay, have you seen Ed?" Daisy asked then.

"Yep, I saw him yesterday too. He's good."

"I'll be back this afternoon Jesse. I need to get busy."

"There's one thing though Daisy. My office will take care of all expenses but right now you better stay away for another few days."

"Well, for God's sake why?" After trying like hell to be calm about things so far Daisy just couldn't keep the irritation at bay and it crowded into her voice.

"Well, sorry Daisy. Right now your lovely bedroom is a crime scene and you don't want to see it. It'll take a few days for the BCA to finish up with their investigations and then they will need to strip it completely; carpet, drapes, and furniture. You will need to redo it, but of course, the cleanup and the cost will be covered by us.

"Oh--, I had no idea," Daisy whispered crestfallen, as she thought about all this.

How long would it take before things would be normal again? Would they ever be right again?

"Jesse," she said then slowly, working on a decision. "You can reach me on my cell, so let me know when you're all done with the bedroom so I can hire a decorator to come in. She's going to love starting with a bare room."

"Okay, I'm so sorry about all this, Daisy," Jesse said with a rumble in his voice. "If you weren't such a lady I would swear a blue streak about all this happening to you."

"Thanks Jesse, but it's not your fault. You know, it all started with my girlfriend Roma's involvement with Gunther Mueller. Which of course was not her fault either, how could she know that he was a hired killer?"

A silent moment passed and then Daisy said to her old friend. "Jesse, thank you again for everything you've done for me and I'll be seeing you soon."

Epilogue

As Daisy sat in her room in a lovely hotel and waited for room-service, she had found she'd had all she could take of the "quiet life" she thought she'd have when she had moved back to Birch Lake. And during her stay in Minneapolis she found she truly loved the city life again.

In those ensuing weeks, the name Bjorn Olafson was found to belong to the second "murder for hire" man, and his body was also flown back across the seas to Oslo, Norway, to be met by the FBI. And after months of investigations his body was finally released to his family for burial.

No one knew for certain if his death marked the end of terror.

Realizing she could never relax in her home in Birch Lake again as she'd always be fearing the reappearance of the snakes, Daisy decided to contact a realtor friend and sell the house, including her manicuring business. And she would look for a new home in a western suburb of Minneapolis.

She called her friend Ed Harrison and they agreed to meet often in the city. She also discussed her life change with her attorney, Reed Conners.

Her finances were such so she could live comfortably regardless of the sales of her properties so she could make the change anytime. And if and when that inheritance from Roma's estate came through, maybe she'd do that special something they had always talked and dreamt about when they had been young and poor, and busy raising their families. Sadness appeared again momentarily as Daisy recalled those days. She wiped her eyes. How exciting it would have been now, if Roma had lived.

Then she stroked Romeo who was asleep in her lap and felt his warmth, and raised a cup of coffee to her lips and sipped at its dark roast while she made her plans.

The end

TO ORDER COPIES OF
THIS BOOK
Please feel free to contact me through
my e-mail at
lindylewis1@msn.com
or my website at
www.Mystery-Novels-Lyn Miller
LaCoursiere.com
You can find my books in soft cover
or e-books on
Amazon.com
NightwritersBooks.com
and Maple Grove Arts Center

Lyn Miller LaCoursiere lives in Minnesota but also spends as much time as possible by the ocean in the south. Lyn has published numerous newspaper articles dealing with life and life's challenges. This is her seventh novel introducing her new character Daisy O'Dell.

Watch for MOONBEAMS TOO
coming soon!